ROSALIE HUDNECKER is fourteen, awkward, dreamy, unsure of herself. She wants to know all the things they don't teach in school: how to look like a movie star, how to grow up easily, how to *live*. Her life seems as stuffy and changeless as Loretta's House of Beauty where her mother works.

Then a trailer home replaces the wooded lot next to their old house on Cedar Street. Rosalie hates the big, ugly metal box. But Jill and Tony Judson, the young married couple who move into the trailer, are beautiful. Rosalie becomes more and more absorbed watching them, their arms linked, talking softly, leaning toward each other. She dreams of being part of their life—the three of them walking along together and laughing, people envying their belonging to each other.

Soon Jill and Tony, as if out of a dream, become her friends—grown-up friends, not like the silly kids at school. In the intensity of her involvement, Rosalie loses touch with her mother, with old friends like Ed and Judy, and with herself as well. As Rosalie realizes that the trailer and its miniature world are not magic—or even all that different— she discovers there has to be more to her own life than just looking on.

Betty Miles' latest novel is funny and heartwarming. Young people will recognize the uncertainty and, finally, the spunky determination that make Rosalie a character to remember.

BY BETTY MILES

A House for Everyone
What Is the World?
Having a Friend
The Cooking Book
A Day of Summer
A Day of Winter
A Day of Autumn
A Day of Spring
Mr. Turtle's Mystery
The Feast on Sullivan Street
Just Think!
Save the Earth!
The Real Me
Around and Around—Love
Just the Beginning
All It Takes Is Practice
Looking On

Looking On

A NOVEL BY

Betty Miles

Alfred A. Knopf

New York

for Sara Miles, with love

THIS IS A BORZOI BOOK PUBLISHED BY ALFRED A. KNOPF, INC.

Copyright © 1978 by Betty Miles
All rights reserved under International and Pan-American
Copyright Conventions. Published in the United States by
Alfred A. Knopf, Inc., New York, and simultaneously in
Canada by Random House of Canada Limited, Toronto.
Distributed by Random House, Inc., New York. Manufac-
tured in the United States of America.
10 9 8 7 6 5 4 3 2 1

Library of Congress Cataloging in Publication Data

Miles, Betty. Looking on.
Summary: Fourteen-year-old Rosalie has difficulty facing
the reality of her own life and finds herself increasingly
caught up in the lives of the newly-married couple next
door. [1. Identity—Fiction] I. Title.
PZ7.M594Lo [Fic] 77-15946
ISBN 0-394-83582-4

1

Bright spring sunlight glittered off bumpers in the parking lot and lit up the store fronts of the shopping center. In the sudden April warmth Rosalie felt uncomfortable in her tights and heavy sweater. Kicking a shopping cart out of her way, she walked between rows of parked cars and came out in front of the upholstery shop next door to Lorretta's House of Beauty, where her mother worked. She set her school books down on the sidewalk bench and pulled a scarf out of her pocket. Looking into the shop window, she tied the scarf tightly over her hair, tucking in the last frizzy strands.

The heat of the sun warmed her back and the thin air smelled sweet. Rosalie looked hopefully at her reflection. She stared at her shadowy image, feeling the same dreamy sensation she had when she walked out of a movie, still smiling the heroine's smile, and wishing she were as mysterious and beautiful.

A car honked behind her.

Rosalie jumped, made a face at her reflection, and rehearsed what she would say to her mother ("The thing is, we have to tell them by tomorrow."). Then she picked up her books, and balancing them against her stomach, walked past the upholstery shop and pushed through the door of Lorretta's House of Beauty.

The row of women under the dryers, sensing the sudden flash of sunlight across the shop's fluorescent pall, stared up at Rosalie together, looked her over briefly, and sank back into their hooded dozes. At her station across the room, Maxine pinned a curler in place on a customer's head and waved with her free hand.

"Hi, Rosie. Your mom's in back, doing a frosting."

After the thin smell of spring outside, the shop's scent of hair spray, nail polish, and hot air seemed heavier than usual. Stepping awkwardly around clumps of hair, Rosalie walked toward the back of the shop. She could feel the eyes of the women under the dryers on her back. Once Rosalie had heard a customer call her "that big, awkward girl of Rita's" and that was how she felt. Not only in the shop—in school she always stared enviously at the small, pretty girls, carelessly aware of their good looks, who bounced through the halls as though they were on stage. Their hair was shiny. In her daydreams, Rosalie tossed her hair around like a shampoo model and smiled at handsome men. In real life, she held the frizzy ends back with a scarf.

Rosalie ducked behind the curtain and went into the small back room, crowded with sinks and storage cabinets. Senoritas and matadors danced across the peeling wallpaper. A coffee machine stood on a metal table, and the smell of coffee merged with the sharp fumes of peroxide. In the middle of the room sat a large woman with a plastic cape over her body and a plastic cover on her head through which clumps of gray hair stuck out.

Rita, in her white uniform and flat white shoes, was bent over the woman, but looked up and smiled when Rosalie entered. Rita was small and angular and her short hair curled in the damp heat.

"Hi, hon. How ya doin'? I didn't expect you this early." She walked around the chair and bent over the woman's forehead. "Let me just finish Mrs. Taylor up, then I can take a little break. Can you hang around for another five minutes?"

"Sure," Rosalie said. "There's this thing from school I have to ask you about."

"Anything wrong?" Rita straightened up.

"Huh-uh. Just something I have to ask you."

Rita brushed peroxide solution onto the last clump of hair, adjusted the plastic cover at the back of Mrs. Taylor's neck, and patted her shoulder.

"There, now. You just relax and dream about how you're gonna look when this is all finished."

Mrs. Taylor clasped her hands across the cape, made a face, and sighed deeply. With the small spikes of hair protruding from her plastic turban she looked like a giant insect from another planet.

"Want a magazine?" Rita asked her. "*Screen Gems? Cosmopolitan? Teen Romances?*"

"No thanks," Mrs. Taylor mumbled. "I'll just grab myself a little nap." She looked at Rosalie with drowsy frankness. "Your girl's sure growing up fast, Rita."

Rosalie hated comments like this, and dreaded those that often followed: "You ought to try her on that new all-protein diet," or, "She sure is well-developed for her age." Rosalie thought if she heard the words "well-developed" one more time, she would scream.

Rita was scrubbing her hands at the sink. "Believe it or not, she turned fourteen last month. Gonna be in high school next year. Got a steady boy friend already."

Rosalie flinched. Rita talked about teen-agers as though this was still the fifties, when she grew up. The phrase "steady boy friend" made Rosalie think of comedy reruns on TV, where cute blond boys tinkered with junky cars. Real life—hers, anyway, and this made her wonder about other people's—was never anything like the shows that were supposed to tell you about it. The boy friends in magazines or movies were nothing like Ed. Ed was thin, with red ears and a blotchy skin. Even if his skin cleared up he wouldn't really be handsome. But the worst thing was that Ed was two full inches shorter than Rosalie. She felt enormous just standing next to him. Still, Ed was a good friend, pleasant and easy to talk to. He talked about interesting things like ecology and politics, even when he wasn't in school. But Rosalie couldn't seem to make Rita understand the difference between Ed and a "steady boy friend."

"Why are you so touchy about it?" Rita would ask when she tried to explain. "It seems like all you want to do is criticize the way I say things."

Mrs. Taylor was still staring at Rosalie. "Tall enough for a model," she said to Rita, as though Rosalie wasn't there. "If she'd just take off some of that extra weight. And let me tell you, now's the time to do it. It gets harder the older you get. Look at me!" She patted her stomach comfortably. "Though to tell the honest truth, I can't say it ever hurt me with the men. There's plenty of them likes a soft pillow." She laughed.

Rosalie was always surprised at the way the customers talked. Sometimes they were just disgusting. But Rita, who would jump on Rosalie for saying "damn" or "stupid," or other things all the kids said, never seemed to be offended.

Drying her hands, she said, "Oh, I keep after Rosalie the best I can. But you know kids, always drinking Cokes and going out for french fries, pizza, greasy stuff."

That wasn't fair, either. Rosalie tried hard to stay away from junk foods. Ed was always talking about the chemicals in them.

Rita went on predictably. "And it's not just the calories, it's what that stuff does to their complexions, too. And the money! With things so tight, it just hurts me to see kids throw away a dollar here, a dollar there."

"That's the truth." Mrs. Taylor nodded her turbaned head knowingly. "But just you try to tell them . . ."

Rita glanced apologetically at Rosalie. "Yeah, well, I have to say this kid's pretty good. She listens to her old mom sometimes, huh, Rosalie?"

Rosalie nodded gratefully.

Rita wound the timer and set it on the shelf behind Mrs. Taylor. "Comfy? You take it easy, now. Enjoy your nap. A real beauty sleep, huh? This is gonna take an hour, at least. Sure you don't want a magazine?"

"I'm half asleep now," Mrs. Taylor said groggily. "You watch, you'll have to come and shake me when the time's up. Go on, have your coffee. Have a nice little visit with your girl."

Rita filled a paper cup from the coffee machine, added a spoonful of sugar, and took a cookie from a box in the supply cabinet. She pulled the cord to the fluorescent fixture on the ceiling. The bright ring flickered and went out.

"Wanna go sit outside a minute? It looks so nice out. I just never got the chance to duck out today, even for a sandwich." She nudged Rosalie. "Look at that. Out like a light."

Mrs. Taylor's eyes had closed. Her mouth hung open and her knees were apart. She was snoring softly.

Rosalie followed Rita into the front room. Two women were asleep under the dryers. Doreen, the afternoon girl, was cutting a small girl's blond hair into a Dutch bob while the girl's mother leaned forward critically from her bench by the window.

"Doesn't she look cute," Rita said, smiling at the little girl. "You have a real gift for styling, Doreen."

The girl's mother relaxed on the bench. Rita could always put customers at ease.

Doreen smiled. "Thanks, Rita. Hi, Rosalie. You two should get out and catch that sunshine while you can. There's a big rush coming up, Rita."

"Oh, boy," Rita sighed. "Seems like it's been rush, rush, rush ever since we got here this morning. Right, Maxine?"

"That's for sure." Maxine shook a can of hair spray vigorously. "But you don't have anyone down till Mrs. Crawford at four. Relax, Rita. Get yourself a sandwich. You ought to eat more than just that cookie, no kidding." She circled the spray can over her customer's head. Rosalie stifled a cough.

"Let me get you something, Mom," she said, holding the door for Rita. "I could run over to the deli real fast."

Rita sank down on the outside bench. She put her head back, stretched out her thin legs in the white stockings, and sighed.

"Oh, I guess not. Why spend the money now when I'll be home to eat in a couple of hours?" She looked across the parking lot. "Look at those trees over there with the little green leaves coming out all over! We oughta be lying in the sun on a day like this, huh?" She patted Rosalie's shoulder. "How'd it go today?"

"O.K., I guess. I got B in my history test, and Mrs. Miller gave back my English assignment, the one about New York. She said it was good. And Judy tried out for the play—for Juliet! I bet she'll make it." Judy was small and thin, with long blond hair and a sweet smile. Just right for Juliet, Rosalie thought, wishing she didn't feel jealous.

"That's nice. I wish *you'd* try out for some show, hon. You used to be so cute in those grade school assemblies. Everybody said. Remember that pink tulip costume with the petals I made you for Mrs. McDowell's spring pageant? I thought I'd never get those petals to hang right!" Rita turned the other side of her face to the sun. Then she sat up. "What was it you said you had to ask me?"

"We had this eighth-grade assembly today. In the auditorium. About our high school programs. They want to make up our schedules. We have to tell them if we're going to take the academic program or the vocational."

"Do you have to tell them right away?"

"I think they pretty much want you to say now."

Rita sighed. "Decisions. There's always something, no kidding. It's the worst part of bringing up kids alone."

Rosalie nodded. It was bad enough having the school after you to sign away your whole life before you knew what you wanted. It was worse to have to explain the procedure to Rita and set her off complaining. Why was everything so complicated, Rosalie wondered? Why couldn't school leave you alone? Or teach you what you really wanted to know: how to be thin and beautiful, to live somewhere interesting, to do exciting work. How to *live*.

A car pulled up in front of them.

"That's Mrs. Crawford," Rita said wearily. "It never fails. Just let me try to grab a break, the next appointment comes early." She stood up and tossed her coffee cup into the trash can.

"We'll talk about it tonight. Not that I know what to tell you," she said grimly.

Mrs. Crawford got out of her car and slammed the door. Then she opened it again and leaned back inside. "I don't want to hear one word out of you, not one little peep," she told the small boy in the passenger seat. "And keep your hands off that horn or I'll come out and give you what for." She slammed the door again, and locked it.

"Kids!" she said, coming toward them. "Whatcha doin' out here, Rita, goofing off again?"

She wore a checked pants suit and high wedge shoes. Her hair looked as though it had just been done. "You ready for me? I'm leaving the kid in the car so he won't get in trouble. I wanna sit in peace under that dryer, for once in my life."

"This is my daughter, Rosalie," Rita said.

Mrs. Crawford looked at Rosalie critically. "Oh."

Rosalie could feel her hair slipping out of her scarf. Women like Mrs. Crawford always made her feel messy, even though she would die before she went around all stiff and lacquered like them.

"What's it going to be today, set and a manicure?" Rita asked.

"I don't know about the manicure, with Billy in the car. You know how kids are. They can't sit nice and quiet and wait for you. If I stay too long he'll be tearing up the upholstery." Mrs. Crawford shook her finger at the car. "Remember, now. Not one single little peep."

Rita held the door open for her and turned to Rosalie. "I never even thought about the shopping, hon. Never mind, O.K.? If I think of something we need I'll grab it on my way home. You could just take that leftover meat loaf out of the refrigerator, maybe cook up some rice to go with it." She waved at the car.

The child stared stolidly out the window. He didn't wave back.

Rosalie followed her mother inside and picked up her books.

"Don't study too hard, kid," Maxine called after her

as she pushed back out into the sunshine.

As she walked past Mrs. Crawford's car, Rosalie bent to look in the window. The child was pulling maps out of the glove compartment. It was going to get hot in there. Rosalie smiled at him, but he didn't look up.

She walked slowly across the sunny parking lot. In front of the Mobil station on the corner, weeds pushed up through the rough gravel curb. The new leaves on the trees and bushes across Route 340 were golden. Rosalie thought about that little kid shut up in his mother's car, and about her own mother, shut up all day in the stuffy beauty shop. She shifted her books in her arms, waited for a line of cars to go past, and walked across the highway.

For now, anyway, she was free.

2

Rosalie walked slowly down Third Street with the hot sun on her back.

Every year this old part of Vandam shrank as the empty lots on its edge filled up with drive-ins. But just a block away from the highway the streets were still lined with trees planted long ago. Birds flew about with bits of straw, making nests as though they were in deep forests. Children ran through the open back yards, and more bikes than cars were parked at the curbsides.

Rosalie turned onto Cedar Street, where she had lived all her life. It was lined with small frame houses with front porches and narrow yards. Most of them had been built fifty years ago, and they had settled solidly into the ground behind plantings of forsythia, lilac, and yew. Maple trees, beginning to show pink buds, arched across the street.

To Rosalie, the most beautiful part of Cedar Street was Mrs. Cree's back lot, next door to her own house, where a group of five tall white pines towered above their soft, needle-covered shade. When she was small, Rosalie had played for hours under the trees, making houses for her dolls in the hollows of their roots, reading Nancy Drew mysteries on quiet afternoons, and playing Kick the Can on blue summer nights with her brother, Joe Pat, and the kids on the block.

Sometimes, she still went next door to read in the woods, as all the kids had called the lot, though Mrs.

Cree had grown deaf and cranky and sometimes asked her to run an errand for a nickel as though she were a six-year-old. Rosalie's bedroom window looked over the woods. When she turned out her light, she could stare out at the tall trunks, black against the moon, and watch moonlight sift through their feathery crowns.

People were always fixing up the Cedar Street houses —adding garages, building barbecue pits, blacktopping their drives. But the street itself looked old-fashioned and comfortable. It seemed permanent and changeless, except for the next block, where the new exit ramp for the Thruway had abruptly cut into it five years ago. Now, instead of the placid white houses that once stood down there, the giant weedy bank of the Vandam exit on the Albany–New York Thruway rose up to the sky.

Rosalie stopped in front of the Majeskis' house to look at the purple and yellow crocuses blooming in a circle on the lawn. A small wooden girl in a painted polka-dot dress and bonnet held her wooden watering can above the flowers. That little wooden girl had watered crocuses in May and gladiolas in July as long as Rosalie could re- member, standing upright in her metal brace while things changed around her: the Thruway exit cutting off the street, the MacDonalds going up two blocks away, the last kids her own age, the Ramsey twins, moving up- state. Mrs. Garrity dying. Her own father leaving them. And now Joe Pat was gone.

Before the Thruway ramp, the Majeskis had a clear view of Carpenter Mountain. From the top of Carpenter you could see all the way across the Hudson, to little white towns spread out on the far banks. Rosalie and Joe Pat used to ride their bikes to Carpenter and climb its ridges, hunting wild blackberries as they scrambled up the rocks. In those days you could ride a bike eight blocks in any one direction and be out of Vandam. Rosalie and Joe Pat had explored the roads together, stopping for Joe Pat to look at every old Chevrolet or Ford behind a barn. Back then, Rosalie had never stopped to think about what her life would be like, even the next day. Now she wondered about it all the time.

Once or twice a year, when summer was thick and hot, their dad had called in sick to the garage where he worked and driven them out to the state park by Newburgh. He would rent a rowboat and take Joe Pat and Rosalie, one at a time, out to fish in the still center of the lake. Rosalie hated the worms and the barbed hooks and the pale slimy fish flopping sadly about in dirty water at the bottom of the pail. But she loved to sit under the hot sun and watch her father, usually an awkward, angular man, standing in easy balance in the boat, casting out shining arcs of line over the water. Her father had never talked much; when he fished, his silence was comfortable and complete.

At home, he seemed a distant spectator while they bustled around him.

"You're not out fishing now!" her mother would yell at him impatiently. "Don't just sit there like a bump on a log. Say something! Talk about the weather, for God's sake!"

Rosalie wished he would ask about her school work, or break up the fights she and Joe Pat got into. But her father just sat in his chair, the paper on his lap, looking at them absently.

In the end, though, he said plenty. He wrote the message on scrap paper before anyone was up one raw winter morning:

"Good-bye, Rita and kids, I am sorry but I can't help it, yr. loving husb. Lamar Hudnecker."

It had turned out that what he couldn't help was running off to Florida with Shirley Eckles, a silent blonde woman who kept the garage's books.

"That no-good, spineless fool!" Rita yelled in fury when she read the note. "No wonder he never said anything, he was afraid he'd let the cat out of the bag!"

She tore the note into little bits and threw them in the garbage. Then she made breakfast for Joe Pat and Rosalie and sent them, shivering with surprise and confusion, off to school.

That was eight years ago, when Rosalie was six, old enough to spell out her father's words before Rita grabbed the note away, but too young to know what the words would mean. It took a long time to find that out, longer than her mother's first tears and rages, longer than the time it took Rita to use up the money her father had left in the bank. When it was gone she begged more from her uncle in New Jersey and went to Vandam Beauty Academy for six solid months, cleaning the place every night after people had left, to help pay for her tuition. That year, when Rosalie came home from first grade with her finger paintings and her workbook sheets stamped with the teacher's stars, it was Joe Pat she showed them to, and Joe Pat's praise she waited for when her mother was too tired to pay attention.

Sometimes Rosalie wondered if her father's leaving had been worse for Joe Pat than for her. He was older; he must have been more embarrassed. Kids probably teased him. But even when they were grown, the two of them hardly spoke of what they'd gone through. For Rosalie, Lamar Hudnecker had faded into a memory of childhood, gone like her first two-wheeler. His absence was a matter-of-fact part of her life, painful only briefly, as when a teacher casually said, "Take this announcement home to your parents," or when she read an advertisement with a picture of a smiling woman and two kids clinging to a tall man, with a caption like "What would they do if you weren't here?"

Rosalie was grown before she realized how much her mother had done, pulling herself together, taking care of the kids, going after the beautician's license and the job at Loretta's. It was there she met Maxine, who bought out Loretta the year Rita started work. Now they were as close as sisters, working together all day and visiting or talking by phone at nights. Maxine was married to Charlie, an easygoing man who liked to putter alone in the basement while Maxine went to the movies or out to Bingo with Rita. Maxine was like one of the family. She praised Rosalie's grades and gave advice on posture and hair care. Rosalie didn't mind. Maxine's good-natured teasing was like a friendly aunt's.

She teased Joe Pat, too. From the time he started to go steady with Joanne Stumpf—she had been his girl friend from ninth grade on—Maxine would ask when they planned to get married.

Joe Pat would say, "Aw, lay off, Maxine," and brush back his hair in a pleased way, while Joanne giggled adoringly. Rita hovered over the two of them anxiously, but Rosalie had hung back, confused at her sense of loss.

Before Joanne, Joe Pat had spent hours around the house, tinkering with the radio or working at his tool bench, wiping dishes for Rita and helping Rosalie with homework. When they had roast chicken for dinner it was Joe Pat who carved, teasing Rosalie by offering her white meat when he knew she wanted dark. His quiet presence had made them seem like a family.

After Joanne, things changed. Joe Pat said, "Cut it out!" when Rosalie tried to tease him. He began to nag

Rita for money and to leave the house abruptly after meals. Sometimes he didn't come home to eat at all. Then the kitchen was strangely empty, and Rosalie and Rita, passing food to each other, talked blankly about the weather or slid into pointless arguments over Rosalie's clothes or hair.

In a way, those two years when Joe Pat was mooning over Joanne and finishing school helped Rosalie prepare for his real departure. Still, she was hurt and surprised when he told them in May of his senior year that he planned to marry Joanne.

Rita was unhappy about it. "How in God's name are you gonna get married without a cent? What's gonna come of your big ideas about owning a garage? You watch, you'll end up stuck in some little place with a bunch of kids and no money and the next thing you'll be walking out on them. Wait a year and see, why don't you?"

But Joe Pat wouldn't wait. And now he was gone, living up in Newburgh with Joanne.

Rosalie reached her house and sat down on the front steps, leaning against the porch railing. Mr. Garrity was pulling up crab grass across the street—his first attack in the yearly war he waged against weeds in his small lawn. Rosalie watched him absently, thinking about Joe Pat.

She was sure of one thing: Joe Pat would never run off from Joanne. She knew he must have a picture of a happy family in the back of his mind, a picture that he was determined to make come true. Rosalie envied him for knowing what he wanted and going after it. He'd done well in the high school automotive course, with three good job offers to choose from when he graduated. Joe Pat said the one in Newburgh had the best chance for advancement, and he took it. Newburgh was fifty miles away. Rosalie wondered if Joe Pat chose that job to get away from them. She still missed him badly.

Everyone said Rosalie looked pretty in the pink dress and picture hat Joanne's family bought her for being bridesmaid, but all through the ceremony she was conscious of how she towered over the bride. Joe Pat, in a ruffled shirt and a suit with a green satin stripe, had laughed and enjoyed himself at the wedding party. He had suddenly seemed more like a distant relative than her own brother. When he and Joanne were cutting their cake, Rosalie had tried to remind him of how he once stole half a cake Rita made for a PTA sale, but Joe Pat didn't seem to remember.

Rita had stood forlornly among the wedding guests in a long blue dress, the orchid Joe Pat bought her stuck to her chest, talking with Maxine and dabbing at her eyes. Joanne's parents didn't seem to mind that she was moving away; after all, they had four other kids. Joanne's mother explained carefully to all the guests that Joanne wasn't pregnant. "Here's two young kids who didn't *have* to get married; they *wanted* to. Isn't that sweet?"

Rosalie thought it was very sweet, but she had gone to bed that night in tears.

After their week in the Poconos, Joe Pat and Joanne found an apartment above an Italian restaurant in Newburgh. They didn't come to visit often; Joe Pat said he had too much overtime. Now Joanne was pregnant. The baby was due in September. It made Rosalie feel more left out than ever. She often day-dreamed about what their life was like, imagining them buying their groceries and making supper, going bowling, sitting on the couch with their arms around each other, watching TV. Being in love.

The house felt empty with Joe Pat gone. Rosalie was

glad when Maxine came over to sit in the kitchen with them. Rosalie's friends said she was lucky to have a mother like Rita, who was so friendly and interested in everything. But they didn't have to live with Rita's complaints and worries. She had long since stopped raging over Lamar Hudnecker, but the hurt he did her had a lasting effect; Rita was painfully afraid that people would take advantage of her.

"Don't take anything for granted," she would say, or, "I'll believe *that* when I see it in writing." She was suspicious of the produce man at the Grand Union, of the town clerk's tax figures, of the Carlsons, for whom Rosalie baby-sat. And it seemed to Rosalie that her mother was suspicious of her, in a way she couldn't help. "Before I know what hits me, *you'll* be gone," she said one day out of the blue, leaving Rosalie with a sudden twinge of excitement and a dreadful sense of guilt.

The sun had left the porch. Mr. Garrity pushed his wheelbarrow, loaded with crab grass, toward the back of his house. Rosalie remembered the meat loaf. She jumped up and went inside.

The smell of breakfast toast still hung over the living room. Rosalie pulled back the flowered drapes she had closed last night when they watched TV. Across from the set was her father's old recliner, with a matching hassock that was lopsided from the way he used to cross his feet. "No use throwing out a good chair just for spite," Rita had said after he left. Now she sat in it most evenings, watching TV, her tired legs stretched out on the hassock.

Over the mantel hung a large oil painting, one of her parents' wedding gifts. Its name was printed on the frame: *A Woodland Lake*. The painting showed a stag with huge antlers standing by a lake. A row of blue and purple mountains rose across the water, and a setting sun dropped behind them. Rosalie had always thought the painting was beautiful. When she was small, the stag had seemed like a loving father, guarding his hidden family in their woodland home. She had stared at him for hours.

But recently the painting had begun to bother her; it was so different from the bright watercolors in silver frames on the Carlsons' white walls. Everything at the Carlsons was light—beige couches, pale green rugs, white lamps with silk shades. Eric's room was white, too, with bright toys arranged on white shelves. Rosalie enjoyed taking them down and setting them out on the rug when she played with Eric. She could almost see Eric's brain working as he invented things for his toy people to do.

"Now the mother's coming down the street," he'd say, "and she says, 'Oh, dear, where did I leave that little boy I brought with me? Never mind, I'll just finish my shopping and then I'll go and find him. Knock, knock, do you sell baby carriages in your store?'"

Then Rosalie would be the storekeeper and ask what kind of carriage the lady had in mind.

"A great big one with lots of room in it," she would say in Eric's high voice, "so my little boy can ride in there with the baby."

Mrs. Carlson was going to have a baby in May or June. She said it was much too soon to tell Eric, but Rosalie was sure Eric knew. He was already explaining things.

"The baby comes out of the mother's stomach," he'd tell Rosalie. "And then the mommy has to go and lie down to rest and then she looks to see if it's a boy or a girl and if it's a girl she's glad."

"She's glad if it's a boy, too," Rosalie said. She loved

Eric. She could hardly bear to think of him feeling left out when the baby came. She worried that Mrs. Carlson would like the baby, boy or girl, better than a four-year-old kid who messed up his toys and spilled juice on his shirt. If she were Mrs. Carlson, she would have explained all about the new baby to Eric by now, and hugged him and told him she would love him just the same. But Mrs. Carlson lay in her bedroom with the shades down and asked Rosalie to keep Eric out of her way. "I just can't seem to stand the noise anymore," she would say, right in front of him.

Rosalie turned away from *A Woodland Lake* and went into the kitchen. She took out the meat loaf, resisting the impulse to eat a bite of it cold. She was trying to use willpower not to eat. But it was hard to be the only person in the family who had to be careful about weight. Rita was naturally thin. So had her father been, and Joe Pat was just plain skinny.

"Don't let *him* get hold of your diet soda," Maxine used to say. "He'll disappear!"

Rosalie wished people could tease her like that, instead of insisting she was lucky to be tall. Being tall wasn't lucky to her. Being big and tall was awful.

The phone rang. It was Judy, excited.

"Rosalie, guess what, I got it! Congratulate me—I'm Juliet!"

Rosalie felt a shock of envy. "That's great. I knew you would, though."

"I can't believe it, honestly. You know who I thought would get it? Chris Newman. I really did. I nearly fell over when Mr. Bloom said it was me!"

"I'm not surprised, though," Rosalie said. "You look exactly right for Juliet. Chris is too old-looking. Besides, she talks through her nose. Who's Romeo?"

"Guess."

"Tommy Geohegan?"

"Guess again!"

"Randy Filler?"

"Billy Kirchener!" Judy shouted. "Can you imagine, 'Wherefore art thou Billy Kirchener?'? But he's good, he really is. Oh, Rosie, we're going to rehearse every single day from now to the performance, and some nights. It's going to be so much fun! I can't wait to tell Mom. Listen, go out for makeup, O.K.? So we can be at rehearsals together? Most of the kids who got parts are juniors and seniors and I feel so nervous with them."

"I'll see," Rosalie said shortly. She didn't like to think about standing backstage with no part of her own except making other people look good. "I have to baby-sit, remember."

"Not *that* much. You wouldn't have to come to many rehearsals anyway. Come on, Rosie. You better decide before somebody else volunteers."

"I'll think about it," Rosalie said. "Listen, I have to go. Mom's going to be home and I haven't fixed supper."

"O.K., see you. I'll tell you all about it tomorrow." Judy sounded exuberant. "Bye, Rosie."

No one would ever pick me for Juliet, Rosalie thought bitterly to herself, putting the phone down. I'm just too big. Too big and fat. She opened the refrigerator and took out a head of lettuce.

Just then, a chain saw began to screech.

3

The sound came from Mrs. Cree's yard. Probably some man she'd hired to clear brush. Rosalie filled the water glasses, folded two paper napkins. The relentless chain-saw buzz grew louder, like a dentist's drill nearing the nerve. Rosalie looked out the kitchen window.

They were sawing into a pine tree! Rosalie rushed outside, nearly stumbling on the steps.

"Hey! Stop!" Frantic, she cut across her yard, pushed through a lilac bush, which snapped back at her face, and came out in the little clearing by the woods. Two men stood there, holding a rope and a gas can, while a third, bending over his saw, made the final cut through the trunk of the pine.

"Stop!" Rosalie yelled toward the man with the gas can. "Make him stop!"

He turned. "What?"

"That's a good tree!" Rosalie shouted. "You can't cut it down!"

The saw gave a final shriek and fell to a low buzz.

"Better move back, girlie, or you're gonna be in trouble. One of these trees comes down on you, it can hurt you bad," the man said.

Rosalie stepped back and watched the severed pine wobble on its stump, tilt, and crash, slowly at first and then faster till it hit the ground in a rush of branches. The man with the saw stepped onto the trunk and walked along it appraisingly.

Rosalie ran up to him. "What are you doing? This is private property!"

He laughed shortly. "You're damn right it is. And you're trespassing. Now just calm down and get out of the way. We don't have time to fool around. Got to take all these trees down before dark."

Rosalie backed off. "You're cutting them *all?*"

"Soon as you get out of here. Come on," he said, turning angry. "This is dangerous work. Move!"

The kitchen door slammed and Mrs. Cree came down the steps, smoothing her apron. "What's the trouble, now?"

Rosalie ran back to her. "The trees!"

"What's the matter? One of those men say something ugly to you?"

"They said they're going to cut the trees!"

"That's right," Mrs. Cree said. "They finally got around to it. I must of called them two, three months ago. Seems like nobody wants to take on a good job these days. Now I don't know how they expect to get through before dark. Should have been here a couple hours ago, like they promised."

Rosalie began to understand. "You *want* them to cut the woods down?"

"Tried to get those trees took down two months ago, so's I could get the trailer set up back here. Though if I knew the trouble I was gonna have with permits and all, I would of thought twice, before I got started."

"The trees—" Rosalie began. A trailer! She couldn't believe it. A trailer back here, and the woods gone! What right did Mrs. Cree have to do such an awful thing?

The chain saw started up: two short bleats, then a steady, throbbing screech. Looking up, Rosalie saw her mother turn into the driveway in her old gray Plymouth.

"Mom!" She pushed back through the lilac and ran to the car. "They're cutting down the woods!"

Rita rolled down her window. "Boy, that's some awful noise! Just what I don't need after a hard day. Come on inside, hon, I can't hear a thing out here."

Even inside the kitchen, with the back door shut, the noise was terrible. Rita sat down at the table and kicked off her shoes.

"I didn't think the old gal would really do it. It makes me sick to think of those trees gone, not to mention some tin box of a trailer back there practically in our yard. I guess I shoulda said something to you way back in December when she started talking about it, but I didn't want you to get upset for nothing. I didn't think she'd go through with it, all the aggravation, permits, variances. But this lawyer she got told her, as long as there's the community college, there's gonna be a demand for housing. I don't know, I guess she needs the money. . . ."

"The woods was the best part of the block!" Rosalie was close to tears. "Why couldn't she leave a couple of trees, anyway? Who's going to want to live on some bare ugly lot without any shade?"

"It won't be bare, hon. There's our apple tree, and the lilac hedge—"

"But the pines! Oh, Mom, that trailer's going to be right on top of us." Taking it in, Rosalie put her head down on the table and sobbed. "Everything keeps changing! Everything good gets spoiled!"

Rita wet a paper towel and wiped Rosalie's forehead. "Some good supper's gonna make you feel better," she said gently.

But the noise of the chain saw, interrupted twice by shouts and the crash of falling trees, kept on as they ate. Rosalie could hardly taste her food.

At last it was quiet. Rosalie cleared the plates and rinsed them off before she let herself look out the window. The ground was piled with trunks and thick green branches, like the aftermath of a tornado. The men stood under the last tree, looking up and laughing.

"The biggest one's still there," Rosalie said.

"They'll probably finish tomorrow." Rita measured out instant coffee. "It's gonna seem strange, with the woods gone. I wonder who she'll find to rent to. I tell you, I wouldn't wish Mrs. Cree on my worst enemy for a landlady. She'll be back there poking her nose into that trailer day and night."

Rosalie felt wrung through. She was still shaken from the encounter with the tree men, the awful sawing noise and the shock of that new raw space where the woods had been. "It just seems like everything's changing," she said again.

Rita put her coffee cup down. "We better talk about what the school wants, hon."

"Oh, yeah." Rosalie got her notebook and took out the paper they had given her at school. It was headed "Selecting a Lifetime Program."

Rita looked it over suspiciously. " 'Dear Parents,' " she read out. "Get that. I'm telling you, I don't see why somebody over at that school can't figure out how to start a letter that doesn't insult you before you begin to read it."

"I guess they just say parents because it's easier."

"Yeah, well, I could tell them a thing or two about *easy*. If they think it's easy, what I've gone through . . . 'Important decisions concerning your son or daughter's future,' blah, blah. They don't have to tell *me* what's important. What do they think I worry about, day in, day out? Your future. Joe Pat's future. *My* future, for God's sake."

"See what they want to know? Should I take the academic program or the vocational."

"They sure come after you fast," Rita said, squinting at the paper. "All of a sudden, and they want you to decide just like that."

"They're making schedules for next year, that's why. I have to tell Mrs. Johnson. I have an appointment with her at ten thirty."

"I'm supposed to figure out your whole future by ten thirty tomorrow? I swear, I'd be happy if I knew what kind of tips I'm gonna make, or if the washing machine's gonna break down, by ten thirty A.M." Rita smiled wryly, patting Rosalie's hand. "Don't let me take it out on you, hon. It's just, there's always something. Now this. What I'd like to say is sure, go into the regular program. You're a smart girl, you make good grades. But that's not so easy to say with a free cosmetology license just staring us in the face if you take the vocational course, worth probably five, six hundred dollars *and* a sure job when you graduate."

Rosalie said carefully, "I don't think I'd be so good at it, though." She paused, trying to choose words that wouldn't hurt her mother. "I don't think I'd like it that much, fixing hair all day." She felt Rita tensing, but she kept on. "It seems so, you know, pointless, all those women trying to be beautiful. Like that Mrs. Taylor. I mean, does she think she's going to turn into *Elizabeth* Taylor just because she gets a frosting?"

Rita exploded. "Listen, Miss Rosalie Hudnecker. If everybody got to do just what they want, you can bet I wouldn't be standing on my feet six days a week trying to please the customers. But nobody ever asked me, would I like to do this, would I like to do that. I had to slave for it. I broke my back to get that license. When I think about those days and how hard it was, all alone and the aggravation with you kids, worrying about sitters. . . ."

She took her cup to the sink and turned the water on hard. "The two of you always needing money for something, teachers after me for parent conferences, assembly costumes. Now you stand there and say you don't think you'd like it. That's not all there is to consider, Rosalie. Like, I wish you even tried to keep your own hair decent. At least somebody like Mrs. Taylor tries to make the best of herself. And I'm glad I can help her, that's the honest truth. I do the best I can, I'd like a little thanks from you sometimes.

"What I'd give," Rita continued, changing direction, "to see you through the academic course, into state university, come out with a diploma and *be* something. . . ."

That was part of the trouble. Rosalie didn't know what she wanted to be, and nobody at school really explained how you choose.

Rita slumped down in a chair. "How'm I gonna figure it out? Anyway, I bet Mrs. Johnson already put you down for cosmetology. Those people up at school try to act like there's some kind of choice, but they have you all figured out before you even say."

"I don't know. Last semester, Mrs. Johnson just asked about you, and about how Joe Pat was doing. I think she put me down on this list, Non-College Bound, but she said we'd talk again. I guess that's tomorrow."

"Can't she give you a little more time before you say once and for all?"

"Maybe. I could ask."

"They sure keep after you," Rita said. "I remember when they signed up Joe Pat for auto mechanics. He was just a kid but they were already going on about annual wages and pensions and supporting a family." She laughed sourly. "And now here he is, up in Newburgh, supporting a family."

"It isn't really a family yet."

"It's ordered, that's the same thing. I tell you, Joe Pat and Joanne aren't gonna know what hit them when that baby comes. Try to tell them, they don't want to hear you. They're gonna get some shock when that baby starts eating three meals a day, getting into mischief. . . ."

"Mom, it isn't even born yet, don't start worrying now! They'll be good parents, I just know it. And you'll be a nice grandmother."

Rita sat up. "Yeah. Grandma. Forty-four years old, a decent figure if I do say it, enough pep to hang onto a job and raise two kids, and what do I get—now I'm gonna be *Grandma*. Not that I couldn't use some of that rocking-chair stuff, but that'll be the day."

The phone rang. Rita jumped up. "That's probably Maxine." She went to the hallway. "Hi, Maxine. Yeah, we just finished. We're sitting here talking about Rosalie's school program for next year. Would you believe they want us to say by ten thirty tomorrow A.M. whether she should go out for the vocational course, take cosmetology, or go on with the academic program and try for college. . . . Yeah, they give you everything right up through the license, you don't pay a cent. . . . Sure, she's smart. But where would I get money for college, outa my tips? You've got to be kidding. . . . Sure, go get it. I'll hang on." She told Rosalie, "Maxine says she just read your horoscope."

Rosalie shrugged and began to wash dishes. She thought horoscopes were dumb. How could a newspaper know you when you didn't know yourself? But Rita and Maxine read them faithfully.

Rita smiled at the phone. "That's pretty good. I'll tell her. Well, see ya, Maxine. You're gonna get some shock the next time you come over here. Old Mrs. Cree took those trees down, out back. . . . Yeah. I hate to think about it, a trailer out back. But what can you do?"

When she had hung up, Rita told Rosalie what Maxine had read from the paper. "It said you're embarking on a difficult period with much success at the end and that perseverance will pay off. How about that?"

"It'll probably be difficult, anyway."

"Oh, for goodness sake, Rosalie, it's gonna be difficult if you *make* it difficult. You gotta have that perseverance it talks about. What you want to do right now is go upstairs and wash your hair so it's nice for tomorrow. Let Mrs. Johnson see what an attractive person you can be. Stand up straight and tell her what you want right out."

"What'll I tell her?"

"Tell her to take her cosmetology program and push it on somebody else's kid!" Rita said angrily. "Tell her to stop trying to run people's lives! Tell her I want my kid to *be* somebody, not stand around in a beauty shop like I have to. You go and tell her I've had all I can take of being pushed around up at that school. They train Joe Pat and what do I get? He's up in Newburgh, fifty miles away." She shrugged her shoulders tiredly. "Ask her if we can put you down for the academic course now, and change next year if we have to, huh?"

Rosalie touched her mother's arm. "I'll ask her, see what she says. Thanks, Mom."

"Don't thank me. It's you that's gonna have to do the work, prove yourself." She smiled weakly. "Want me to wash your hair for you down here in the sink? A real professional shampoo?"

"That's O.K., Mom. You worked hard enough today. Go and watch some TV."

"O.K., but wash it good, now. And put out a nice clean blouse for tomorrow." Rita went into the living room, turned on the television, and settled into Lamar Hudnecker's old brown chair. An hour later, when Rosalie came down to say good night, she was asleep.

Before she went to bed, Rosalie stood at her window and stared out at the strange new clearing where the woods had been. The last pine tree, its thick crown black against the dark sky, stood alone above the fallen trunks and piles of brush. The woods had always seemed so far away and secret. Now the exposed lot was close and strangely bare.

Rosalie tried to imagine a trailer back there, stuffed into the small lot. Who would want to live there, practically right under their windows? If she wanted, she realized, she could watch everything they did. They wouldn't have any privacy at all. And from now on, neither would she. No soft, cool woods to sit in, alone, thinking her own thoughts and looking up at the sky.

No more woods! She didn't know how she could bear it.

4

In the clear morning light, the lot looked worse. It was cluttered with trunks and brush, gouged with tire marks, scrubby and open and raw. Even the surviving tree was stripped bare along one side where a felled trunk had scraped against it. Rosalie brushed her hair hard, fighting a helpless rush of unhappiness. From now on, she would have to look at this view every day. And it was going to be worse.

She tried to describe it to Ed as he waited with her outside Mrs. Johnson's office.

"It's so empty and bare-looking. It doesn't even look like there'll be room for a trailer. I just hate to think of having people living back there."

"It's a crime to cut trees like that," Ed said. "I bet those were the oldest pines in Vandam. Just wait—every empty lot in town's going to be filled up with trailers."

"Not where you live," Rosalie said. "But nobody cares about Cedar Street any more. Look at the Thruway ramp." Suddenly she thought of the old, peaceful view of Carpenter Mountain. "It seems like our whole block's spoiled."

Ed looked at the wall clock. "I better go, Rosie. Have a good interview."

"Thanks."

Ed leaned over. For a minute Rosalie thought he was going to kiss her, but he was only reaching for his book. Rosalie was embarrassed at her thought. She always envied the easy way grown people kissed each other. She wondered how you ever got casual about it.

"Don't let the old bag push you around," Ed told her.

Mrs. Johnson came out of her office, frowning as though she'd heard him. "Rosalie Hudnecker?" she said into the air, reading the name from her list as though it had no connection with a real person. Sometimes Rosalie wished it didn't. She hated her name, and the way she had to spell it out to everyone. She longed for an easy name like Smith that no one could stumble over.

"That's me." She stood up, wondering if she was supposed to shake hands. But Mrs. Johnson turned and led the way into her cubicle. It was made of glass walls that stopped short of the ceiling, so people outside could hear anything you said.

Mrs. Johnson consulted her list. "I see I have you down tentatively for the cosmetology program."

"Well, that's not really what I want," Rosalie said.

Mrs. Johnson looked up impatiently. "What do you have in mind? We must have come to some agreement last fall."

Rosalie was sure she didn't remember that interview. "I said I didn't really know. Maybe you put me down for it because my mother's a beautician?"

Mrs. Johnson seemed grateful for the cue. "Oh, that's right." She shuffled through folders on her desk. "Now I remember. Your mother works at Loretta's, right? And your brother went through our auto mechanics program. How's he doing now?"

"Fine. He's married. He has a job in Newburgh."

"Isn't that nice. So you know firsthand how successful our vocational graduates are. Some of the courses we offer you'd pay hundreds of dollars for on the outside. That's not something to pass up lightly, in your position."

"I know. But my mother and I decided I should try the academic program. For a while, anyway. And then, if it didn't work out, I could go into cosmetology."

Mrs. Johnson frowned. "That seems like a roundabout way to select a program. We like to feel students have a serious commitment from the start."

"Oh, I'm very serious." Rosalie leaned forward. "See, I don't want to work in a beauty shop all that much. I'd like to try some other things."

"What other things do you have in mind?"

"I'm not sure, yet. I don't really know."

"How are your grades?" Mrs. Johnson pulled a transcript from the folder and scanned it hastily. "I don't see anything very outstanding here."

"I have about a *B* average," Rosalie protested.

"You'll need at least that, to get through the academic program. It's quite stiff, you know. You say your mother wants you to go on to college? Does she know anything about the cost of a college education these days? Perhaps I ought to talk with her."

Rosalie was determined to forestall a meeting between them. "She knows it costs a lot," she said, wondering how much it actually did. It couldn't be that bad at Carpenter Community.

"Well, I'm too rushed right now to argue, though I may regret it later. We'll put you down for academic, with a 'tentative' after it. But remember: it's not easy to change from one program to another in midstream. Still, you'll have to change if you can't keep up." She put down the folder. "Do you have any outside interests, Rosalie?"

"Well, I baby-sit for this little boy—"

"That's fine," Mrs. Johnson said approvingly. "Clubs?"

"Drama Club," Rosalie said.

"Good." Mrs. Johnson stood up, to show her the interview was over.

Judy and Pam were in the hall.

"Where've you been?" Pam asked. "We needed you in gym. Our team lost."

Volleyball was one of Rosalie's talents. Her height was an asset on the court, and she had a powerful serve. But it was a coed class and she was always aware of her large thighs beneath the red legs of her gym suit. She never minded missing gym class.

"I had to see Mrs. Johnson about my program."

"What did you tell her?"

"Academic. Mom said I should. I don't think Mrs. Johnson thought it was such a good idea, but she put it down. So now I'll get to be with you guys." She felt suddenly reprieved. It would have been awful to have to go way out to Newton School every afternoon, just to learn about hairdos! "But I don't know what I'll major in. It seems like all I know is what I don't want."

"You don't have to decide all that now," Judy said, just as Ed had said earlier. But both of them did know what they wanted: Judy was determined to be an actress, and Ed was going to work in ecology.

"Coming to rehearsal today?" Judy asked. "They're assigning the last parts and setting up crews."

"I can't. I have to baby-sit."

"Want me to say you're interested?"

"Sure." Rosalie knew she'd feel unhappy on opening night if she did makeup, watching Judy put on some fabulous costume. Still, the backstage crews had fun.

"I'm working on costumes," Pam said. Pam was a genius at sewing. "Did you learn all your lines yet, Judy?"

"I'm working on it." The bell rang and people began to push into classrooms. "It's hard, but the play's so beautiful! I'm scared I won't be good enough."

"You'll be great," Rosalie said enviously. Judy was so lucky to be small and pretty—and talented. She wished she was good at something. The thought nagged at her all day.

But after school, ringing the Carlsons' doorbell and hearing Eric running to answer, she felt better. She was really good with Eric.

"I'm coming, Rosalie, I'm coming!" he shouted from the other side of the door, struggling with the latch. Then he pulled the door open triumphantly and jumped into her arms.

"Hi, Eric." Rosalie gave him a squeeze.

"You know what?" he started in. "A lady just won a hundred candy bars!" Eric loved to watch game shows on television; he never seemed interested in the regular children's programs. "And another lady won a boat with four bunk beds! I wish I had a boat like that." He made a steam-whistle noise.

Mrs. Carlson appeared, hugely pregnant, in a quilted robe and high-heeled slippers.

"I want you to turn that television off right now," she told Eric. "Hi, Rosalie. Eric's had the volume on that set going full-blast for the last hour, so I couldn't get to sleep. I don't know why he can't learn to keep it down. He drives me crazy with his TV!"

Rosalie smiled at Eric. "We'll do something quiet together, O.K., hon? Color, or do a puzzle?"

Eric pulled at her sweater. "I want a glass of milk and a jam sandwich. Come *on*, Rosalie."

"Don't talk to Rosalie like that," Mrs. Carlson scolded. "Say 'please.'" She and Rosalie followed Eric into the kitchen. "I'm sorry it's such a mess." Mrs. Carlson waved at the counters covered with dishes. "I just didn't seem to have the energy to get to it. Get a snack for yourself while you fix Eric's. I'm going back to bed for a while." She picked up a copy of *Vogue* from the kitchen table and clumped out.

"I'll get the milk," Eric shouted. He pulled a half-gallon carton from the refrigerator and held it over a small glass. The milk quickly spilled over, running onto the table.

"Be careful, Eric." Rosalie got a dishcloth and wiped it up. "You should have waited for me. What if your mother saw you spilling milk like that?"

"She'd spank me," Eric said matter-of-factly.

Rosalie wiped up the milk, poured a glass for herself, and made two peanut butter sandwiches, one for each of them. She set Eric's in front of him, smoothing back his blond bangs. His forehead was smooth and perfect. His blue eyes looked out from dark lashes. He slurped his milk, filling his cheek and squishing the liquid from side to side. In a minute, he'd probably laugh and spit it all out. Rosalie loved him.

"What did you do today at nursery school?"

"Nothing."

"You must have done *something*."

"At circle time Emma said she was going to have a baby sister." Eric looked at Rosalie over his milk glass. "She brought a doll to school. You know what? It pees out of its stomach! What a dumb doll." He wiggled in his chair, still drinking. Milk dripped onto his shirt.

"Be careful," Rosalie said. "You have to learn to drink like a big boy, not a baby."

"I don't drink like a baby. Babies drink out of bottles. I don't drink out of a bottle, so I'm not a baby."

Rosalie finished half her sandwich and started on the other. She knew peanut butter was terribly fattening. If only it didn't taste so delicious!

Eric pushed his plate away. "I don't like crusts."

"Come on, just try them for once. It won't hurt you."

Eric picked up his sandwich by the corner and dangled it over his plate.

"I don't want it."

"O.K., we'll save it in case you change your mind later." Rosalie took his plate, envying Eric's lack of interest in his food.

She began to stack the dishes in the dishwasher.

Eric slid out of his chair and hugged her knees. "Let's go do my firehouse puzzle."

"When I'm done with these dishes."

Eric grabbed her sweater.

"Careful, you'll stretch it."

He gave the sweater a jerk. "I wanna do the puzzle now!"

"Let go!" Rosalie said, exasperated. "I'll be done in a minute." He must be tired; he wasn't usually so impatient.

Eric sat down at the table and pushed his empty milk glass around. Rosalie put knives and forks in the dishwasher, closed it, and wiped the counters. She loved this kitchen when it was clean. Mrs. Carlson had such pretty baskets for bread and fruit. Shiny copper pots hung from the wall. The stove and refrigerator were copper-colored, too. At home, the stove was white, with black scars where the enamel had chipped off.

"Are you going to have a baby, Rosalie?"

Rosalie hung the dishcloth over the faucet and turned to face him. "What do you mean? Someday, or what?"

"Are you having one now, I mean."

"Of course not. Where'd you get that idea?"

"Because your stomach's so fat."

Rosalie was hurt. "It's not *that* fat. It's nothing like your mother's." She caught herself. "I mean, just because a person's stomach is big, doesn't mean they're going to have a baby."

"Sometimes it does."

"Sometimes it doesn't." Rosalie took out a broom and swept the floor, not looking at Eric. He picked up his feet so she could sweep under them.

Then he grabbed the broom handle and looked at her challengingly.

"Anyway, Mommy's having one."

Rosalie felt trapped. What was she supposed to say now?

"Mommy's having one," Eric said again, waiting.

Rosalie lifted him off his chair and slid onto it beneath him. She settled him in her lap and brushed his hair back.

"Listen, Eric, I'm going to tell you something, a special secret. I guess your mommy didn't tell you yet because she wants to surprise you. But you know what? She *is* going to have a baby, someday. A little brother or sister that you can play with. And when you don't want to play with it, then you and I can do things together, just like we do now."

Eric reached up and poked his fingers over Rosalie's chin. "I know," he said, resignedly.

"You'll like it, wait and see." Rosalie wished she hadn't told him, but how could she have avoided it? He didn't seem to be shocked, but he sat quite still on her lap.

"Will it be a girl baby?"

"That's the thing; nobody knows what a baby will be till it gets born. It's like a surprise. Maybe it will be a girl, maybe a little baby boy, like you were." She squeezed him and sang into his ear: "Oh, you must have been a beautiful baby. . . ."

Eric wriggled off her lap.

"Mommy doesn't like boys." He reached for his discarded sandwich and took a bite.

"Yes she does. She likes *you*. She liked you when you were a baby and she likes you now. Now that you're so big and grown up and go to school and everything."

Eric threw his crust onto the table. "I'm going to go tell Mommy about the baby!" He ran out of the kitchen.

"Eric!" Rosalie whispered loudly after him. "Come back! Don't bother your mommy while she's napping. Come on back!"

But Eric ran down the hall, twisted the doorknob of his mother's room, opened the door, and went in.

Rosalie finished sweeping the floor, listening for sounds from the back of the house. In a few minutes Mrs. Carlson came into the kitchen. She looked tired.

"Did you just tell him?"

"I'm sorry, Mrs. Carlson. He kept asking me things and I didn't know what else to do."

"You shouldn't have taken his questions so seriously. His teacher told me, just last week, he never even mentions babies at school. Now I'm afraid he'll be worrying about it all the time." She leaned against the wall.

"I'm sorry. But I really think he already knew."

"Oh, I know you didn't mean anything wrong," Mrs. Carlson said. "It's just—I've been dreading having to tell him." She laughed apologetically. "I don't know what's the matter with me."

"Maybe—would you like me just to go home now?"

"I guess that's best." Mrs. Carlson reached into a drawer and counted out Rosalie's money. Don't feel bad," she said. "It isn't your fault; it's my problem."

But Rosalie did feel bad. Mrs. Carlson had paid her as much as usual and she'd only stayed an hour. And what if she'd done something that would make Eric's adjustment difficult? She walked home slowly, feeling sorry for him and for Mrs. Carlson and for herself.

Turning onto Cedar Street she suddenly remembered the woods. She walked to the back of her house, knowing what she would see.

The last pine tree was down.

5

The woods were gone forever. It took very little time to change that thick, shady space into a small, exposed lot. For two days men swarmed over it, measuring and digging and putting in stakes. They carted truckloads of brush away, and a bulldozer tore out the last few bushes, leaving them to wilt on the flattened ground. Mrs. Cree ran in and out of her house, pointing the workmen's cars away from what was left of her grass. Rita made ominous comments about what it would be like with people living back there. Rosalie tried to stay away from the window, as though not watching would keep it from happening. But on the third day, when she came home from school, the trailer was there.

It was worse than she could have imagined.

The trailer was small, but it filled the small lot from end to end, with only a strip of bare ground, not even enough to call a patio, in front of it. It looked like a big metal box that had been painted to suggest a house. There were red window frames and red shutters, and a metal chimney that was painted red and white to look like brick. An ugly silver tank was attached to a network of pipes at one end. There was a tall television antenna on the roof. Wires ran from the front of the trailer to a raw wood pole that towered above the hedge of scraggly lilac between the yards. Shiny and bare on the bare lot, the trailer was so solidly *there* that it made everything else in the two back yards—Mrs. Cree's clothes dryer, the

Hudneckers' apple tree and bushes—look small and un-familiar.

"I hate it!" Rosalie said at supper time, staring blankly out the kitchen window.

Her mother sat at the kitchen table with Maxine, who had driven over to see what was happening.

"It makes the back look like some kind of shantytown," Rita said, looking out over her coffee cup.

"Well, people have to live somewhere," Maxine said. "A nice little trailer makes a good home for a young couple just starting out. You take Joe Pat and Joanne—they'd probably like a trailer all their own instead of an upstairs apartment."

"Yeah, but we don't even know it's gonna *be* a couple," Rita said, spooning out a dish of Jello for Maxine. "It could end up two girls, maybe even three, taking it. And who knows what kind of people? Just about anybody who comes along could sweet-talk Mrs. Cree into renting to them."

"What's wrong with two girls?" Rosalie asked, trying to imagine real people walking up those cinderblock steps.

"You watch. We get a bunch of girls out there, the next thing it'll be boys traipsing through the yard after them, parties, noise, maybe a fire—"

"Oh, Mom, don't start worrying yet." Rosalie was suddenly excited. It might be fun to have a bunch of girls move in. Maybe she could even go over and visit them.

Maxine said, "Hey, Rosie, I brought over the new issue of *Hairdo* with a cute style in it that made me think of you. Want to see?" She rummaged in the plastic shopping bag she carried everywhere, pulled out the magazine, and turned to the picture.

"Look at that."

The heading of the page was "Teen Tresses." All the girls in the photos looked like cheerleaders. Maxine pointed to the picture of a blonde with curly bangs and a pinned-up pony tail.

"Isn't that cute?"

"*My* hair wouldn't go like that."

"Wanna bet? Let me cut you some bangs and you'd see. They'd curl up just like hers. I think you'd look real nice, Rosie."

Rita bent over the magazine with professional interest. "It's hard to tell what kind of texture that hair is. I don't know if Rosalie's would curl under like that."

"With a little set—" Maxine began.

"I don't *want* a hairdo you have to set," Rosalie said quickly.

Rita looked up, annoyed. "Yeah, it's hard enough just getting her to brush hers. You might as well give up, Maxine, she won't try something new. It's like talking to a wall. And here she is with the two of us all ready and willing to work on her hair any time she wants. For free. A lot of girls would give anything to be in her shoes."

"I know it, Mom. It's just that I don't want some kind of hair *style*. I just want plain hair."

"Plain hair's fine if you'd keep at it, brush it a hundred strokes a night, don't let it frizz up the way yours does."

Maxine pushed the magazine back into her bag. "It's O.K. I know she doesn't want a lot of advice from old fogeys like us. But just remember, kid, any time you get the urge for a haircut, just come right over and head for my chair. I'll give you a cut that even you'd have to admit was cute."

"I asked Ed for supper tomorrow night," Rosalie said to change the subject. "He wants to see what they did to the woods."

"That's nice," Rita said approvingly.

"I saw this story in the *Enquirer* today," Maxine said. "About Princess Whatshername running off to London with a boy her mother doesn't approve of. So you should be glad, Rita, that Rosie likes to bring her boy friend home."

"Yeah, well, she better not think about running off with him!"

"Mom!"

Maxine laughed. "Don't put ideas into her head!"

"Don't worry," Rosalie said. Ed wasn't the kind of tall, mysterious man you would dream of running off with. He was just a boy she liked.

Still, she blushed the next day, remembering this conversation, when Ed put his arm around her on their way home from school. He had to reach up to do it. His arm felt nice, even though Rosalie almost had to limp to keep in step with him. It was pleasant to walk through town like this in the late afternoon, while the sky around them turned pink. The maple trees on Cedar Street had softened with pink buds. The street was quiet, but Rosalie looked down it toward Mrs. Cree's driveway and saw people moving about.

"Hey, it looks like people are moving in!" she said, excited.

There was a VW van parked in Mrs. Cree's driveway. When they came nearer they saw three men and a girl pulling shopping bags from the back of it while Mrs. Cree walked back and forth among them, waving and pointing and wiping her hands on her apron.

"Want to stop and watch?" Ed asked.

"Oh, no!" said Rosalie quickly. "We can see them from the kitchen. Come on." She led him inside, where they could watch everything without being seen.

"Wow, they sure have a lot of stuff," she said, looking out the kitchen window.

One of the men had a beard. He seemed to be directing the others. Rosalie noticed right away that the girl was tiny. She stumbled down the driveway carrying a huge suitcase that bumped against her legs at each step. When she reached the trailer door she lunged up the cinderblock steps, pushed the suitcase inside, and turned back to the van.

They can't be very old, Rosalie thought. Mrs. Cree must have got students like she wanted. "I wonder which ones are going to live back there," she said. "It would be funny if it turned out to be two boys. Mom never thought of that."

"That would be pretty interesting for you."

"Oh, Ed!" It would be interesting, Rosalie thought. But she didn't want to say so. "Look at that plant! It'll be as high as their ceiling."

"That's a dracaena," Ed told her. "They don't need much light. You can stick them in a corner anywhere."

They watched the people carry a chair, some cushions, a small table, and several cardboard boxes into the trailer, while Mrs. Cree looked on anxiously from the driveway. The girl leaned into the van and pulled out a long striped skirt on a hanger. She draped it carefully over her arm and took it into the trailer.

"The girl's going to live there," Rosalie said.

"With how many of the rest of them?"

"Oh, Ed! She's probably married to one of them and the others are helping them move."

"You can't be sure. Maybe they're going to have a commune or something."

"In one little trailer?"

"Who knows?" Ed laughed. "Hey, what's for supper?"

"Oh, I forgot! I'm sorry," Rosalie said. "Hamburgers, and beans, and salad. Is that O.K.?" Ed's family usually had fancier meals, complicated casseroles or stews.

"Sure," Ed said. "Sounds good. I'll help."

They shaped the hamburger patties, and Ed cut up salad greens while Rosalie set the table. She looked up frequently to see what was going on outside. There were lights in all the trailer windows. It looks sort of nice, she thought with surprise, watching people's shadows move across the yellow windows. She wondered what it was like in there.

Rita drove up. She got out of the car and stood by the door, looking at the trailer. Then she came inside.

"That's some gang over there," she said. "I hope to goodness they're not all going to live there."

"I bet it's just one couple, and the others are helping them move," Rosalie said. "How was work, Mom?"

"Same old thing," Rita said. "Hello, Ed. I didn't mean to ignore you, it's just that I was surprised to see all those people back there." She went on to Rosalie, "That old Mrs. Weber gave me a quarter tip! I don't know what to say to that woman, I think she thinks she's being generous."

"Want me to make salad dressing?" Ed asked.

Rita smiled at him. "You're certainly handy around a kitchen. Your mom must've trained you pretty good."

"I like it," Ed said comfortably. He always acted natural with Rita, not formal or stuffy the way some kids did with adults.

It's nice to have him here, Rosalie thought. It's like when Joe Pat was still around. She wondered what Joe Pat and Joanne talked about when they got supper. It would be nice if Joe Pat told her stories about home, or said, "Me and my sister used to—"

Ed was telling Rita about a summer school program at Cornell for high school students. He had already applied to go for next year. Ed was like that, sure of what he wanted to do and knowing how to do it.

"Cornell, is that an expensive school?" Rita asked. "What do they charge you to go to a place like that?"

"I think about twenty-five hundred a semester," Ed said. "It'll probably be more by the time I go."

"Twenty-five hundred dollars! You're kidding!" Rita said, startled. "Boy, they must think people are loaded, if they ask that kind of money."

Rosalie wondered how she could go to college if it cost that much.

"They have scholarships, though," Ed said. "And, anyway, there's lots of cheaper schools. Look at Carpenter Community. You could go there for practically nothing if you lived at home."

"Practically nothing, that's more like it," Rita said. "But they'll find a way to hit you for something. Books, fees, carfare . . . nobody's giving away a college education these days."

Rosalie listened without speaking. What point was it being in the academic program if she couldn't even afford to go to college when she graduated?

There were footsteps on the back steps.

Rosalie jumped up and opened the door. A bearded man, one of the people who had been moving things into the trailer, stood outside. He was tall and very thin. He wore a dirty T-shirt and stained jeans. He smiled at them tentatively.

"Hi. I'm Tony Judson. I just moved in next door. Into the trailer next door."

Rosalie caught herself staring at him. Imagine, somebody like this moving into the back yard and coming over here! She thought he looked like a movie actor.

"I don't want to bother you or anything," the man said, looking at the plates on the table. "It's just, we've been over to Mrs. Cree's so many times, and the last time she didn't answer when we rang. . . ."

"Probably went upstairs and couldn't hear you," Rita said. "She takes that hearing aid off, you could blow a siren under her window and she wouldn't know it." She pushed her chair back. "Come on in, be introduced, now you're here. This is Ed, my daughter's boy friend. This is my daughter, Rosalie. I'm Rita. Rita Hudnecker."

Tony stepped into the kitchen and shook hands with Ed. Then he looked right at Rosalie and smiled. "Hi."

"Hi," Rosalie said.

Tony's smile was friendly and a little shy. Maybe that's what got to Mom, she thought. Rita didn't like to ask strangers inside the house. "No matter who they say they are," she often warned Rosalie, "don't let a person you don't know get their foot in the door."

Tony's feet were well inside the door. He leaned against the sink, looking around with frank curiosity.

"It's a nice place here," he said. "I like your back yard, too, with all those bushes and the big tree. It's kind of bare over where we are."

Rosalie felt as though she should apologize. "There used to be these really big trees there, only Mrs. Cree got them cut down so she could put in the trailer. . . ." She stopped, embarrassed. After all, it wasn't his fault about the trees.

"Oh—" He worked out her meaning. "Oh, man, you people must feel bad about that. Hey, I'm sorry."

"It's not your fault," Rosalie said quickly. She could tell that this man wasn't the kind of person who would go around cutting trees down.

"Yeah, but still . . ." He turned to Rita. "What I wanted to ask is, we have all this trash from moving in and I wondered if somebody comes around to collect trash in the morning. I don't want to dump it out unless they're going to pick it up."

"Twice a week," Rita said. "Not till Saturday, now. And they have the nerve to ask six-fifty a month for it."

"Oh, do you have to pay extra? I thought maybe the town did it free. Where I used to live they did."

"Not Vandam," Rita said. "They hit you for everything here. Where you from?"

"Strassberg. My wife's from North Carolina, though. She just moved to Strassberg last year, with her family."

He said "my wife" as though he liked the sound of it. "We got married at Christmas," he explained. "This is our first real place." He paused as though he was waiting for their congratulations.

"Well, congratulations," Rita said. "I have a son just got married last year, too. He lives over in Newburgh. Joe Pat."

It's funny, Rosalie thought. Joe Pat gone, and now here's someone else moving in.

Ed stood up to fill his water glass. Rosalie couldn't help noticing how short and young he looked next to Tony. He was just a boy; Tony was a grown man. With a beard. And a wife. Living in a trailer. I bet they'll have fun back there, she thought, suddenly envious. Just the two of them.

"Well, I didn't mean to interrupt your meal," Tony said. "I better get back. Anyway, it's nice to meet you. Now that we're neighbors." He went to the door.

"Nice to meet you," Rita said.

Rosalie caught herself hoping that Ed wouldn't be there the next time he came.

Tony opened the door and they heard a call across the back yard. "Tony?"

"That's Jill," Tony said in a pleased tone. "After me again." He jumped down the steps two at a time. "So long," he called back.

"He seemed nice enough," Rita said.

"Yeah," said Rosalie. Turning her back on Ed and her mother, she went to the window and watched until Tony's white T-shirt disappeared. The lights in the trailer gleamed warmly. In the twilight, its walls were a dull silver, and the bare ground in front of it had turned purple.

It must be wonderful to be them, Rosalie thought, all alone in that trailer. She was surprised by her sudden yearning to run out of the kitchen, leaving Ed and her mother behind, and stare through the little windows of the trailer.

6

Every day spring progressed a little farther, softening the outlines of trees, turning the grass a bright green, filling the air with leafy smells and sudden streaks of music from car radios. The unfolding spring heightened Rosalie's growing absorption in the trailer the way music underscores a slow-motion movie scene.

At first, she had stared out the kitchen window, or from her bedroom, with no more than ordinary curiosity as Tony and Jill went in and out of the trailer with books or plants or grocery bags. She thought they were a beautiful couple: tall, thin Tony with his thick reddish hair and beard, almost a foot taller than tiny, small-boned Jill, whose fine brown hair hung straight to her shoulders. They dressed almost like twins, in T-shirts and jeans. Jill's were always pulled in at her small waist with a thick leather belt. When it was cool, Jill wore a huge red sweater that made her look even tinier, and Tony wore a jeans jacket like the men in cowboy films. Rosalie loved to watch them come down the steps in the morning with books in their arms, talking all the way to the car and leaning toward each other, laughing, as they drove away. Rosalie wondered what they talked about. She was too far away to catch more than the laughing tone of their voices.

After those first few days, Rosalie realized that her observation had become less casual and that the trailer, which she had resented so deeply before the Judsons moved in, had become an important part of her own life. She worked out the pattern of the Judsons' schedules and began to wait eagerly for them to appear.

In the mornings she hurried out of bed to watch them toss their books into the car and drive off, and in the afternoons she stood by the window waiting for the sight of their car in the driveway. She was glad when her mother was late getting home from work, so that she could stare at the Judsons without having to explain her preoccupation to anyone. She wouldn't have known how to explain.

Sometimes after supper, Tony and Jill ran outside and threw a Frisbee around their cramped space, laughing and taunting each other as they bumped into the clothes dryer or the lilac bushes. Once, when Rosalie was watching them from her bedroom, Jill had missed a catch and the Frisbee had floated up toward her window before it veered and wobbled to the ground. Rosalie had ducked back quickly. Tony had pushed through the bushes and retrieved the Frisbee—for an instant, Rosalie had thought he would call to her and ask her to come out and join them. But of course he hadn't even known she was there.

In the evenings the Judsons watched TV. Rosalie could see the flickering blue light through their windows, and their shadows crossing in front of it. At about eleven, the yellow lights that made the trailer look so warm and inviting went dark. Then, when she could see only a dim metal shape, Rosalie stared out at it, imagining Jill and Tony in bed with their arms around each other.

Now, looking out her bedroom window on a sunny Saturday morning, she remembered how she and Joe Pat used to envy Superman's X-ray vision.

"You know what I'd do if I had it?" Joe Pat had said

once, laughing. "I'd look into the teachers' bathroom and watch Miss Haley do a b.m. on the toilet!"

Rosalie had thought that was the funniest thing she ever heard. After that, whenever Miss Haley came to class to teach songs like "Cielito Lindo" and "Over the Meadows," Rosalie had nearly burst from held-in laughter. Once, Miss Haley commented on her "pleasant singing expression" and Rosalie had got the hiccups from embarrassment.

The trailer stood blank and silent in the morning sun. If she had X-ray vision right now, Rosalie thought, she would look right through the walls and see everything. She wasn't sure what she wanted to see—dishes in the sink? food in the refrigerator? clothes in the closet? rumpled sheets on the bed? books and papers on the table? What else? Flushed, she turned away from the window and began to sort the pile of laundry on her bed.

Rita was at work. "A job with Saturdays off, that's what I call luxury," she always said. On Saturdays she left for work earlier than usual and came home later, exhausted.

The doorbell rang. Rosalie went downstairs and found Judy at the door.

"Hey, Rosie. I thought I'd come for a visit, that is, if you're not busy." She stood in the doorway expectantly. "I'm dying to tell you what's been happening with the play and everything."

Rosalie was glad to see her. "Come on upstairs. I'm sorting out laundry and stuff in my bedroom." She wondered if Judy would look out the window.

"Isn't it nice out?" Judy said. "Remember how we used to ride bikes on Saturdays?" She followed Rosalie upstairs, sighing importantly. "Now it seems as though I don't have time for anything except the play. Honestly, they act as though we don't have any private life at all."

She flopped down on the pink bedspread.

"How's it going?" Rosalie found it was difficult to show a real interest in the play. School things like that seemed suddenly childish.

"It's so much fun." Judy tucked her hair behind her ear. "It's like, when we start practicing, I can hardly remember anything else outside the play."

Rosalie nodded. She understood what Judy meant. That was how she felt, absorbed with Tony and Jill until nothing else seemed important. She wanted to tell Judy about them, but she didn't know how to begin.

"You should have seen us," Judy said. "We had to go through this scene about ten times, where I'm lying on the floor and Billy's supposed to say how awful it is that I'm dead. All of a sudden I saw this wart on his neck—I couldn't stop staring at it. I nearly died!"

"It sounds like fun," Rosalie said. But it sounded sort of silly, too.

"Oh, it is. I love it. I don't know how I'll get my work done—I may fail all my classes and have to go to summer school—but it's worth it. You should see the dress Pam's making: pink satin with black ribbon trim. The top's cut so low! I don't know what Mom'll say when she sees it." She laughed. "I guess you can get away with anything, when it's Shakespeare."

"What's happening with makeup?" Rosalie felt obliged to ask.

"Chris Newman came to the last rehearsal and said she'd do it. I told her you'd probably come and help out when she needed more people. Did she call you yet?"

"No."

"She will. She'll have to have a crew; she can't do it all by herself. So far nobody else I know of turned up to volunteer." She sat up and poked Rosalie lightly. "Be sure to do it, O.K.? I'll feel so much better if I know you're there. There's going to be a neat cast party after the last performance."

"I will." Rosalie was not at all sure that she would want to go to a cast party. Judy was her oldest, best friend, but it suddenly seemed as though they were living in different worlds. "See, it seems like there's a lot going on. Exams coming up, baby-sitting, I have a paper due. And then, you know, the trailer."

"What's the trailer got to do with it?" Judy stood up and looked out the window, frowning. "Boy, is that disgusting out there. It looks like it's right on top of you." She turned. "Have you met the people who moved in?"

"Yeah." Rosalie felt as though she had known them for ages. "I met the man. He came over last week. And I see them both all the time." She glanced out the window, but no one was there. "The man's so nice. You should see him. He must be about six-two, and skinny. He has this reddish beard and red hair, sort of thick and curly. Too bad he's already married." What a dumb thing to say—and it wasn't even true! Being married was part of what made Tony and Jill so fascinating. She had never been so close to people in love before.

"What's she like?"

"She's so cute! I didn't meet her yet, but I see her outside. She's small—she must be shorter than you, even." Rosalie sighed. "How come tall men always seem to like short women? It isn't fair."

"Sometimes short men like tall women," Judy said. "Look at Ed."

"I know it, you dope, but that isn't the same." For a moment, Rosalie felt like her old silly self, gossiping with Judy. "It should be, but it isn't. I always feel so big with Ed. Even my feet are bigger!"

Judy laughed.

"You can laugh, but it's not so funny to me." Hearing a door slam outside, Rosalie turned to the window. "Quick, Judy, look! There they are!"

She waited expectantly for Judy to admire the Judsons. But Judy looked out without noticeable interest and only said, "They ought to make a garden out there, it's so ugly around there now. I feel sorry for you, having to look at it."

Outside, Jill sat down on the trailer steps and stretched her bare legs in front of her. She was wearing very short shorts. Tony sat down next to her and hung his arm casually over her shoulder.

"Love birds," Judy said. "You sure have a good view of them from up here."

Rosalie stopped herself from explaining just how good the view was, and how her window seemed like a frame through which she saw Tony and Jill acting like characters in a movie. She wondered if Judy would be shocked if she knew how many hours she'd spent looking out at them.

"Is that their VW?" Judy asked.

"Yeah, isn't it cute? Don't you think that's a neat color?"

"I don't know, it looks like ordinary VW blue to me."

Judy didn't even seem interested. She was looking through the box of cosmetic samples on Rosalie's dressing table.

Rosalie stared out at Tony and Jill. They were leaning back on the steps with their faces toward the sun. Their eyes were closed.

Rosalie suddenly remembered the dream she had been having when she woke up this morning. She and Tony and Jill had been walking down a sidewalk, their arms linked, laughing together. People were staring at them enviously, and Rosalie woke up suffused with a happy sense of belonging that had lasted for a moment after she opened her eyes.

Judy held up a small tube. "What's this? Some kind of eye shadow?"

"Yeah. It's a sample my mother brought."

Judy squinted and drew a blue-green line above her eye. "You ought to try it. You have such neat eyes."

"Thanks." Judy was always so straightforward. She didn't give compliments unless she meant them. Rosalie wondered if she'd look older with eye shadow. She had noticed that Jill never wore makeup.

"Rosalie!" Judy said. "Stop staring out the window like that! What if they saw you?"

"I'll just finish the clothes." Rosalie moved away from the window. She hung Rita's uniform carefully on a hanger and carried it into her mother's bedroom. Then she hung up her own shirts and put a pile of underwear away. Tony and Jill were still stretched out on the steps. They'd probably look marvelous with tans.

"*Rosalie!*" Judy dabbed at her eyes with a tissue, wiping off the makeup. "I bet they'd be pretty surprised if they knew you were watching them so much."

"Yeah. I have a pretty good view if I wanted to spy on them or something," Rosalie said, trying hard to sound flippant and unconcerned.

As though they had heard, Jill and Tony stood up and went into the trailer, shutting the door behind them.

"I bet they have fun back there," Judy said boldly. "Making love whenever they want to."

"Yeah."

"Did they just get married?"

"Last Christmas. They lived in Strassberg, but she used to live in North Carolina before that."

"How old do you think they are?"

"I don't know—twenty, twenty-one, something like that. He looks older because of the beard."

"I think beards are sexy, don't you?" Judy asked, as though she could read Rosalie's mind.

"Yeah. They make people look sort of sophisticated, I think."

"Except—remember Buddy Crundon, he graduated last year? I saw him the other night at MacDonald's. He had this funny beard. It was all thin and scraggly so you could see his bad complexion right through it."

"I think you have to be good-looking to start with, before a beard looks right," Rosalie said. She had decided this the night Tony came over.

"I'm going over to Grand Union this afternoon," Judy said. "They have an ad for part-time checkers. I don't know if they'll take you under sixteen, though. What're you doing this summer?"

"Baby-sitting, for Eric and the baby, when Mrs. Carlson has it."

"When's it due?"

"It was supposed to be June, but the doctor said it might come early. You know what I did, Judy? I told Eric about the baby. I had to—he kept asking and asking and she wouldn't say anything."

"He probably knew anyway. I read that kids always know, somehow. Is he jealous?"

"He's worried, I think. He acts sort of upset about it. He's so sweet—I just hate for him to feel bad."

"He's lucky to have you," Judy said in her direct way.

"You're so good with kids. I bet he really loves you."

Rosalie was touched. "Yeah, I think he does." She glanced outside. In the light breeze, apple blossoms fell to the ground. It was so nice out there—why shouldn't they sit in the yard? There was nothing wrong with that. And then maybe Tony and Jill would come out, so Judy could see them close up. Maybe, with Judy right there, she'd have the nerve to say Hi, and make conversation about the weather or something.

"Hey, Judy, how about making sandwiches and taking them outside?" she asked, trying to sound casual.

"Sure!" Judy said. "Do you have peanut butter?" She laughed. "It's got to be peanut butter and jelly, the way we always made them. Remember how we used to put on so much jelly it squirted out when we ate?"

"And Joe Pat always stepped in what we dropped on the floor and tracked it through the house." Rosalie laughed, remembering. She and Judy had been friends for such a long time.

They went downstairs to the kitchen. Rosalie found a jar of peanut butter and pulled the jam out of the refrigerator.

"I shouldn't do this," Rosalie said, spreading the peanut butter thickly. "It's so fattening. But, oh, man, I really love it. I'll go easy on the jam, to make up."

Judy giggled. "Yeah, teen-agers aren't supposed to dribble jam on their T-shirts."

They put the sandwiches on paper napkins, grabbed an apple each, and went outside.

"Oh, it's so nice today," Rosalie said, looking around. "Isn't the grass pretty with all those apple petals on it?" It's too bad the Judsons don't have a tree like this, she thought.

"I really miss the woods, though," Judy said. "I just

can't believe that they're gone." She looked at the apple tree. "Want to climb up and eat up there?"

The two of them had spent many Saturdays in that tree. Looking up, Rosalie saw that from the tree they would have a clear view of the trailer. "Sure. I'll climb up first and you can pass me the stuff."

She grabbed the lowest branch of the tree and hauled herself up, bracing her sneakers against the trunk. She looked out at Judy through the leafy branches. "Come on. It's really nice up here."

Judy reached up and handed her the sandwiches. Then she stuck an apple in her back pocket and jumped unsuccessfully for the bottom branch.

"I can't make it! You're so lucky to be tall!"

For once, Rosalie wasn't annoyed. "If you can catch onto the branch, I'll pull you on up."

Judy jumped again and hung on. She braced her feet against the trunk and walked them up. Rosalie stuffed the sandwiches in a notch above her head, leaned down, and pulled. Judy grunted, straining, and heaved herself up. Then they both leaned back comfortably and looked around. Rosalie glanced quickly at the trailer. She wondered what Tony and Jill were doing inside. It was impossible to see through the windows.

"It feels just how it used to up here," Judy said. "All leafy and private." She bit into her sandwich. "It even tastes the same. Isn't it funny how tastes make you remember things?"

"We always used to take peanut butter sandwiches to the lake with my father," Rosalie said, suddenly remembering that.

"Was he nice?" Judy asked hesitantly. "I can't even remember him, you know? Mom said I shouldn't ask about him, but I always used to wonder."

"He was O.K." Rosalie didn't want to make herself sad from happy memories. "The thing was, he ran off. With this woman."

"Oh, Rosie, that's awful! How did you bear it?"

"I missed him. But then I got used to it. It was worse for Mom. She must have been so ashamed. And she didn't have any money when he left. Joe Pat and I didn't really know how tough it was for her."

"Where did your father go?"

"Florida."

"Do you ever hear from him?"

"Huh-uh. Not since the first year. Mom got a divorce and he just stopped writing."

"Wow." Judy took another bite of her sandwich and chewed it thoughtfully. "People shouldn't get married unless they're going to stick together through everything, I don't think."

"That's easy for you to say. Your parents like each other. Mine hardly ever talked, most of the time."

"Anyway, I'm not getting married for years. Not till I'm really sure."

"Well, some people are sure right off," Rosalie said, thinking of Tony and Jill. *They* must be sure. She looked over at the trailer, shining in the noontime sun. It was going to be hot in there pretty soon, with no shade to cool it off. Summer would probably be awful, unless they got an air conditioner. But Mrs. Cree wasn't likely to provide one. Maybe, if they planted vines . . . that's what she would do, plant morning glories and squash and things that grew fast. Then there would be green leaves outside the trailer windows. The phrase "a leafy bower" came into her mind. She must have read it in a book. That's just what they should have, she thought, a leafy bower. Instead of a hot tin box.

The trailer door slammed and Jill came out. "I *am*," she shouted. "I'm getting some rags out of the car."

Rosalie and Judy leaned back into the apple tree so they wouldn't be seen.

Tony came out after Jill. "You can't do it with rags. You have to have a mop."

"Since when are you the big authority on mopping floors?" Jill turned angrily. "Go on and watch your old game. I'll clean up while you sit and relax."

"Come on, don't be mad," Tony said easily. "I just want to see the first inning. Then I'll go get the beer and stuff."

"O.K." Jill said, walking toward the car. "Do what you want. Just be sure you have it all here before everybody comes, that's all. Don't expect me to fix everything right in front of your friends, in that little tiny kitchen. I don't want to get stuck like that."

"For God's sake, nobody's coming till *eight*," Tony yelled. He went inside, slamming the door behind him.

Judy looked at Rosalie. Rosalie couldn't believe what she had heard. It had been almost like a fight. She wished that Judy hadn't been here at all. If only she could see them on the steps in the evening, talking so lovingly!

Judy whispered, "Maybe we should get down before they see us."

"We'd make too much noise getting down. Let's stay till she goes inside. I don't think she'll see us through the leaves." Rosalie felt hurt. It was as though Tony and Jill had betrayed her in front of her friend. Why did they have to pick this afternoon to have a fight?

Jill went into the trailer, slamming the door as Tony had done. The volume of the television inside flared up so loudly that Rosalie and Judy could hear every word of the razor-blade commercial. Rosalie hoped they'd make up before their party.

"Come on!" Rosalie slid down the tree and jumped. She held out her arms. Judy crouched, slid, hung onto the last branch, and then jumped toward her, landing lightly in the grass. They went running inside together.

In the kitchen, Judy turned to Rosalie and giggled. "I'm sure they didn't see us. Anyway, they were too busy arguing to notice anything."

"Yeah." Rosalie felt terribly disappointed. "I never heard them talk like that before," she said. "Most of the time they act so happy." She wanted to take Judy's mind away from what they'd heard. "Remember how we used to hide in the apple tree and spy on Joe Pat and his friends? Remember the dumb club they used to have?"

"Yeah." Judy laughed. "They thought they were so great! All they ever did was sit around and tell each other their password." She washed her hands in the sink. "I better go. The Grand Union manager's supposed to start interviewing at two. I'll see you soon, Rosie. This was fun. Come over to my house next week, O.K.?"

"Maybe," Rosalie said. It was fun to fool around with Judy. It felt like old times. But she was reluctant to go anywhere now, in case something should happen out back. "Anyway, you'll be busy with the play."

"Not that busy. Guess who I'm going to the movies with tonight?"

"Who?"

"Billy Kirchener!"

"Are you crazy?" Rosalie couldn't imagine going anywhere with Billy Kirchener. He was such a kid.

"He's not that bad. It's funny, when you're in a play with someone, you sort of can't help liking them," Judy said seriously.

Rosalie wondered what it would be like to be in a play

with Tony and Jill. Or in a movie. The three of them, arms linked, walking down a street in soft focus. The way they were in her dream.

Judy stood at the door. "So long," she said, going out and running down the steps. "See ya."

Rosalie waved, her eyes on the trailer. She wondered who would be coming to their party.

The phone rang.

"I just wanted to say, Rosalie," Mrs. Carlson said, "that all in all I think it was a good thing you told Eric what you did. You must have said it just the right way. I think he's acting, well, sort of relieved. He does love you, Rosalie."

"I'm glad," Rosalie said.

"I know it's awfully late to ask you," Mrs. Carlson went on. "But would you be able to come over and sit tonight? John and I thought we might go out and see a movie. Anything to take our minds off all this."

Rosalie hesitated. It wasn't fair. Her mother and Maxine were going to Bingo. Ed's family was celebrating his mother's birthday. Judy would be going to the movies with Billy Kirchener. And Tony and Jill would be having a party.

"I'm sorry, Mrs. Carlson," she said, surprising herself as the words came out. "I can't. I'm going to a party."

7

Rita came home exhausted from her Saturday in the shop, and they ate their supper in silence. Throughout the meal, Rosalie was acutely aware of the trailer door slamming and the car backing out of Mrs. Cree's driveway. By seven o'clock it had made four trips in and out. The last time, Rita looked up from her coffee, irritated.

"What the heck's going on over there? You'd think they'd want to plan better, not waste their gas on all that driving in and out." She stood up and looked out the window. "Looks like he's carting in enough beer to last the two of them all summer."

"They're having a party."

Rita looked at Rosalie quickly. "How do you know?"

"I mean, I bet they are. It's Saturday night."

Rita took her coffee cup to the sink. "That'll be the test. I have to say they haven't made much commotion up to now, except for that car. I never realized how lucky we were that Mrs. Cree doesn't own a car. It's a real aggravation, with the driveway so close." She turned to Rosalie. "But you watch, when those kids start throwing parties, having their friends in at all hours, it's going to be a lot worse than just car noise. Music, beer, drinking, fights—I don't wanna think about it."

"They probably don't even have that many friends yet, just moving here from Strassberg. Anyway, they're quiet; they wouldn't like noisy friends." Rosalie hoped deeply that this was true.

"I'll believe it when I see it." Rita took the coin purse from her pocketbook and held up some folded bills. "Look at this—lightning struck twice today. Mrs. Alfrink gave me two-fifty for an eight-dollar condition treatment and set and then old Maggie Phillips coughed up three dollars for her permanent." She counted the bills. "Thirteen dollars altogether, probably more than I ever took in on one Saturday. I'm gonna have myself a nice little fling at Bingo, maybe treat Maxine, too, for a change. What with her always driving me there."

On Saturday nights Maxine regularly took Rita to Bingo while Charlie stayed at home playing poker with his friends. Maxine and Charlie had been married twenty years, fond of each other the whole time. Maxine attributed this to the fact that they spent many nights apart. "Absence," she liked to say, "makes the marriage last longer." Rosalie always thought it was nice of her mother not to point out that absence had ended hers.

Rita gave Rosalie a five-dollar bill. "You take that, hon, before I go and lose it on Bingo. Put it toward a nice pair of summer sandals. I bet you're going to need them. It's a sure thing your last year's pair won't fit you, the rate your feet are growing."

"Thanks, Mom." Rosalie wished, and immediately felt guilty for wishing, that she had the new sandals tonight. "What about you, though? You ought to have a pretty new pair of summer shoes."

"What would I do with a pretty new pair of shoes?" Rita asked matter-of-factly. "Wear them to the shop? To Bingo?" She looked down at her old black shoes, fraying at the heels.

"You know something? I was always vain about my feet. Size four, that's what they call model size." She leaned against the sink, blocking Rosalie's view of the trailer. "I remember when my mom let me get my first pair of heels. I must have been about your age; those days nobody's mother would buy them real heels until they were grown. Now you see little eight, nine-year-old girls teetering along on those crazy wedges, it turns your stomach. Anyway, I picked out a pair of patent-leather shoes with pointy toes and little spindly heels. Mom said I'd fall down the steps as soon as I went out in them. She didn't want me to buy them, but she let me have my way. And I never did fall down. I walked so careful at first, hanging on to everything, but once I got the hang of them you should have seen me dance—right up on those little wobbly heels. Oh, boy, that was something!"

"I wish I had size-four feet," Rosalie said, thinking of Jill's. They must be about that small.

"Stop that kind of talk, Rosalie," Rita said, exasperated. "I get sick and tired of it sometimes, you mooning around about things you can't change. I just wish you'd put some of that energy into things you *can* do: take care of your hair, lose some weight, tuck your shirt in!" She waved at Rosalie's baggy jeans and the shirt that didn't quite meet them.

"Maxine's going to help me make up a pants suit we saw in the Simplicity catalogue. It oughta turn out real nice if she helps me get the hang of the pants straight. I could never sew up a crotch straight by myself, I know that without even trying. Maybe we could make up a nice pair for you if it works out, how about it?"

Rosalie was sure she wouldn't want the kind of pants her mother and Maxine would want to make for her. She had seen them in pattern books on pert, tiny models: double-knit bell-bottoms with sewn-in creases. Nobody at school wore clothes like that. Even Jill, who looked like the pattern catalogue models, wore jeans.

A car honked outside. Rosalie jumped, thinking about the party, but Rita said, "There's Maxine, on the dot as usual."

She dropped her coin purse into her bag, fluffed up her bangs, and pressed her lips together to spread the lipstick around.

"Have a nice night," she said. "You gonna watch some TV?"

"Probably. Maybe do some social studies homework." Rosalie was surprised that just even thinking about the party in back could make her feel so guilty. She wondered if her mother sensed her confusion.

But Rita was following her own thoughts. "Don't study too hard," she said, her hand on the doorknob. "After all, it's Saturday night." Cautiously, she pressed on. "You ought to have some other boys to take you out on dates, when Ed's busy. Maybe you're scaring them off, going steady with him. You don't want to limit your chances."

"Mom! It's *you* that calls it going steady, not me!" Of all things to bring up at a time like this, Rosalie thought. "It's not as though hundreds of boys are hanging around waiting to ask me out," she said. "Anyway, nobody has dates anymore, the way you think. Just because that's what you used to do. People have parties these days, not stupid dates."

Rita was hurt. "Believe me, I'm only raising it for your own good. I don't like to go out and leave you sitting home on a Saturday night, that's all." She stood at the door, looking at Rosalie almost pleadingly.

The car honked again.

Rita opened the door, waved, and yelled out. "Hey, Maxine, hold your horses, will ya?" Her voice was bright. Rita came to life on her short weekends, squeezing the most out of small pleasures like playing Bingo, sleeping late, reading the Sunday paper. Now she ran down the back steps lightly, her tiredness forgotten.

Long ago, when she was so young she asked what she wanted to know, Rosalie had questioned her mother about getting married again.

Rita had snorted. "One thing I'm not about to do is rush out and look for more trouble. You won't catch me waltzing off with the first thing in pants that comes around."

A couple of times after she became friendly with Maxine, Rita had gone out with some friend of Charlie's, or with one of the salesmen who brought beauty products to the shop. Several years ago she had spent some time with Mr. Garrity when he came back to Cedar Street alone after the Florida vacation on which his wife had suddenly died. But one night after an Odd Fellows dance, Rita had flopped down on a kitchen chair and said she was through.

"Mr. Garrity is a gentleman. There's plenty of women who would jump at what he has to offer—a nice house, security, he'd be awfully good to you. But I can't see myself spending the rest of my life playing bridge and making coffee cake for his cronies. I just can't do it."

As it happened, no other woman took Mr. Garrity up on his mild offers. He had sunk into comfortable bachelorhood, tending his house and yard, now and then stopping Rosalie on the street to ask after Rita.

It would be awful to live with someone just for the convenience of it, Rosalie reflected after Rita had gone. She cleared the table and filled the sink with soapy water, her eyes on the window. But it must be wonderful, she thought, to live in your own place with someone you really love.

Jill came out of the trailer with a bag of garbage, put it into the trash can by the steps, and stood there waiting as Tony drove up in the car. He jumped out carrying paper bags, ran up to Jill, and kissed her lightly. They went inside. Rosalie wished Judy could see them now.

She washed the plates slowly, hoping someone would drive up the driveway and go into the trailer. It was nearly eight; surely the party would begin soon. She tried to imagine herself inside the trailer, looking thin and grown-up in some neat outfit, chattering easily.

"Oh, I live right next door," she imagined herself saying, with a little laugh. "I keep my eye on Tony and Jill all day long."

She wiped the silverware, dried off all the pots and put the dishes away. Maybe the guests couldn't find Cedar Street? There was no street sign for it out on 340. What if they all forgot about the party, or just decided not to come?

In one part of her mind, Rosalie felt almost convinced that somehow she would go to this party. In the real, common-sense part of her head, she felt sick with embarrassment for even dreaming of it. What would they think, Tony and Jill and their friends, all of them at least twenty, if some big awkward eighth-grade girl walked in the door? Everybody would stare at her. What could she possibly say? Tony and Jill would hate her for making a scene and ruining the very first party in their new place. She was crazy even to think of it.

"I'm crazy," she said aloud, and felt better immediately. She squeezed out the dishcloth, hung it carefully over the faucet, and put the detergent away under the sink. She pulled a dead daffodil out of the vase on the table and threw it in the trash. Then she rearranged the flowers that were left, patted the tablecloth smooth, pushed the chairs under the table, and went upstairs.

Standing in front of her closet shelf, she studied her T-shirts: the one with the Empire State Building on it, the navy blue Vandam High School shirt, her new tie-dyed green and white one. The tie-dye was the most interesting, she thought, and it went with her white jeans, the ones that were cut full so they didn't pull over her thighs when she sat down.

She tried to imagine herself sitting in the trailer, but she couldn't imagine what she'd say. If the friends were from Strassberg they might like to know about Vandam. But all she could think of was second-grade history about the Dutch settlers, the Onderdonks and Van Meters, whose names were everywhere in town. Or the Blauvelt House, famous for the biggest fireplace in the Hudson Valley, where they used to roast whole pigs.

But nobody at the party would want to hear stuff like that. Maybe she could tell about the trails on Carpenter Mountain. Someday she might take Jill and Tony there to pick blackberries. They could pack a lunch and spend the whole day. . . .

Dreamily, Rosalie took off her dirty clothes and pulled the tie-dyed T-shirt over her head. Just to see how I'd look, she told herself. If I was going over there. She looked in the mirror and made a face at herself. "Crazy," she said again, out loud, forcing her hair down with short hard pulls of her brush. She felt very strange, almost helplessly unable to predict what she would do next; whether she would walk downstairs and turn on TV, or whether she would somehow manage to walk out back and go to the party. Her heart was beating fast, and she felt a shivery kind of thrill, like the ones she got from watching horror movies.

A motorcycle suddenly roared down the street, coming closer and closer until it coughed to a stop in front of Mrs. Cree's.

Rosalie ran to her mother's room and looked down. Two people in white helmets and denim jackets straddled the bike, bracing it against their legs. The front rider pointed down the driveway, revved up the engine, and bumped the bike heavily toward the trailer. Rosalie ran back to her own window in time to see the riders— a heavy-set man and a skinny girl—pull off their helmets and walk clumsily, adjusting to land, toward the trailer steps. Then the door opened, letting out a sudden glow of yellow light against the pink twilight sky. Jill came out and leaned against the doorway. In what seemed like slow motion, the two riders climbed up the steps, paused in front of Jill—the man kissed her—and went inside the trailer. Jill followed them, closing the door. Rosalie felt shut out.

Restlessly, she picked up her hairbrush and began to brush her hair, counting the strokes. In the darkening room, she could barely see the reflection in her mirror. It was possible to imagine that the face she made out, glowing in the pinkish light, was beautiful, with its large dark eyes and pale skin. Rosalie brushed languidly, tilting her head up like a model. She tried out a model's smile—seductive, mysterious, confident. Then she put down the brush and switched on the light. When she looked in the mirror again she saw her ordinary self, big and frizzy-haired, a junior high school kid. Not even a ninth grader, that people might pay some attention to. Depressed, she rummaged in the closet for her sneakers, put them on, and went downstairs.

She turned on the television set and waited for the picture to appear. The sound came first, blasting out a floor-wax jingle. Rosalie adjusted the volume, went to the kitchen for a glass of diet soda, settled down into the brown arm chair, then jumped up quickly as she heard a car turn into the driveway next door. From the kitchen window she saw the VW van that had been there on Jill and Tony's moving day. The same man who had helped with the moving got out of the driver's seat. Two people climbed from the passenger door: a short man and a blond girl—taller than he was, Rosalie noticed—in a white dress.

This time Tony opened the door. The new people vanished inside before Rosalie could take in more than the white dress and the laughter.

It was darker outside now, the deep blue of a warm spring night. Rosalie flicked off the kitchen light and stood with her elbows on the edge of the sink, looking out at the trailer windows. Shadowy figures moved across them. Shrill studio laughter poured from the living-room TV. Rosalie imagined that, by staring very hard, she could hear the real laughter of Jill and Tony's friends as they settled down for a long, easy evening.

Rosalie couldn't figure out what was funny about the comedy that jumped across the television screen, although the laugh track exploded after every sentence. Images of the party in the trailer filled her head so she could barely focus on the screen. She tried to study a Coke ad that came on with a blast of music. Blond girls in bikinis and boys with striped surfboards chased each other energetically across a beach, holding their soda cans toward the camera. Rosalie wondered if scenes like that really happened anywhere. Maybe in California. She knew with certainty that if she looked like one of those girls, she would never in her whole life feel shy about going to a party.

The comedy began again. Rosalie jumped up and

turned it off abruptly. The laugh track hung in the air for an instant as the picture faded into a bright dot in the center of the screen, and then vanished. Now the house was quiet, except for the rattle of the refrigerator, which ran on almost full-time, night and day.

In a sudden rage, Rosalie ran to the kitchen and kicked it, hard. Then, shaking with determination, she pulled her T-shirt down over her stomach, smoothed back her hair, opened the kitchen door, and went outside.

8

I'm not really going over there, Rosalie told herself as she went down the steps. I wouldn't dare. But she kept walking. She felt like an image of herself in a dream—vague, unreal, waiting for the flash of relief that comes from waking to find everything ordinary again.

A thin moon was rising over the apple tree. Coming closer to the trailer, Rosalie was still unable to see beyond the light and the moving shadows into the room inside. She heard a heavy bass thump that meant music was playing. Then Tony's head—she was sure it was his—appeared in the window, bent down, listening. It was like a signal.

Rosalie searched the lilac hedge for an opening where she could get through. She found an open space between two trunks, pushed aside some leafless stalks, and surprised at how easy it seemed, crawled through to the other side. Some twigs snapped at her as she straightened up and stood still, her heart beating fast, with nothing between her and the side of the trailer. It shone palely in the moonlight. Now that there was no place to hide in, she felt queerly invisible, as though her very daring made her safe.

Even close up, the trailer looked unreal. It could almost be a small ship floating across Mrs. Cree's back yard, with the people inside it travelers sailing toward a foreign land. Rosalie was breathless, yet she felt quite peaceful. She wondered if this was how little children in stories felt when miraculous visions crossed their paths, accepting them with calm pleasure and no sense of fear.

Then Tony raised his head and seemed to look straight out the window at Rosalie. Instinctively she stepped back into the lilacs, slipped, stubbed her toe, grabbed wildly at a thin branch that snapped off, reached for another and missed, moaned out "Oh!" and fell, scratching her face on a sharp twig before she hit the ground and lay there in a confusion of pain and horror.

The trailer door opened. Music blared out. Jill stood at the top of the steps, looking down.

"What's going on?" Someone called from inside.

Gasping for breath as the pain in her toe lurched over her body, Rosalie watched Jill walk slowly down the steps. There was nowhere to go. With a crazy sense of relief, Rosalie pulled herself to her knees and stood up, brushing at the dirt and grass on her jeans. Her toe throbbed steadily. Choking with pain and shock, she took a step toward Jill and said the only thing she could think of.

"Hi."

"Oh, hi?" Jill said tentatively.

Rosalie rubbed at the scratch on her face. Her shoe was caught on a low branch. The pain in her toe echoed in the pit of her stomach.

"My shoe came off," she said.

"You must be Rosalie," said Jill.

"Yeah." Rosalie tried to smile. Her face stung. There was a hole in her shirt where it had caught on a branch. She wondered if she would go on standing there forever.

"Did you want something, or something?" Jill asked. She sounded hesitant but not unfriendly.

"Not really." Rosalie wanted to die.

"We're having this sort of party. I hope we weren't

making too much noise or anything."

"Oh, no!" Rosalie protested. "It's not that. I couldn't hear a thing till I came out. Honestly."

Behind them, the music rose to a higher pitch. Rosalie bent down and freed her sneaker. Hanging onto a branch, balancing on one foot, she tried to push the other into the sneaker. "I'll just put my shoe back on," she explained.

Tony came to the doorway and looked out. "What's going on?" Then he recognized her. "Oh, hi, Rosalie. I didn't know it was you. How ya doin?"

"I fell," Rosalie said. She was too numb to invent a reason for being there.

Jill said, "Come over and sit down on the steps and put your shoe on." She spoke in a soft, rhythmic way that Rosalie recognized as southern. Despite her confusion, she was charmed by the sound of Jill's voice.

She limped to the steps like a sleepwalker in a bad dream, horribly sure of what was going to happen: they would ask her to come inside. How *could* she?

Someone yelled again, "Hey, what's up?"

"Just the girl next door," Tony shouted back.

The words made Rosalie feel better. The girl next door was such an ordinary thing to be. She sat down on the bottom step and worked her foot into the sneaker. Behind her, music throbbed.

Then Jill said, "Hey, are you doing anything? I mean, right now? Why don't you come on in and see our place?"

Like an obedient child, Rosalie followed her up the steps, aware of her throbbing toe, her torn shirt, the tangle of twigs in her hair. Jill stepped into the trailer, but Rosalie stood back, confused by the light and the music and people staring up at her. She caught her breath, afraid that she might cry.

"Come on in, Rosalie," Tony said.

She stepped into the room.

Tony pointed to the people. "Buddy, Cheryl, Ken, Lisa, Bill. This is Rosalie."

"Hi," Rosalie said, feeling huge and awkward and stupid in front of them.

But the people said "Hi" and turned back to each other, picking up glasses, reaching for chips.

Tony walked to the kitchen for a plastic stool with metal legs and carried it back above people's heads to a spot next to Lisa, the girl in white.

"Sit," he said, smiling at Rosalie.

Rosalie sat.

On the stool, she was much higher than anyone else in the room. She felt horribly conspicuous, aware of her torn shirt and her throbbing toe and her awful reason for being there at all. She had crashed the party. And this wasn't some kids' party where everybody crashed. This was a real party.

But no one seemed to notice her embarrassment. The man called Buddy took a long drink of beer and banged his bottle down on the table.

"Got another one of these things?"

Jill took a beer from the small refrigerator and gave it to him. "How about you, Rosalie?" she asked. "Want a Coke?"

"Thanks," Rosalie said gratefully. She never drank beer. Rita kept some in the back of the refrigerator for Maxine, but didn't touch it herself. Rosalie wondered if this was the kind of party where people got drunk. What would her mother say? What would her mother say if she knew Rosalie was here at all? She sipped nervously at the Coke Jill gave her. With the glass in her hand she felt a little less conspicuous. Trying not to stare, she looked around her, taking in the room she had only imagined before.

She thought it was the most beautiful room she had ever seen, it was so colorful and snug and cozy. Yellow light fell from little shaded lamps on the walls onto bright pillows and curtains and floor cushions. There was an orange and yellow spread over the couch and another on a small table in the kitchen part of the room. The tall green plant she'd seen when they moved in filled the corner beside the couch, and there were little plants in pots on all the windowsills. There were bookshelves made out of bricks with boards across them, only partly filled with bright new books. A poster of mountains and sun hung above the couch, and a woven cloth strung with beads and fringe was tacked over the bookshelves.

The little kitchen—it was all part of the same room— was cluttered with yellow dishes and bright ceramic bowls, and the small stove and sink and refrigerator fitted neatly into the narrow space. Candles were burning everywhere.

Through the haze of smoke and music and laughter, Rosalie stared at Tony and Jill. They sat close together on the couch, holding hands. It's like watching a play, she thought; if only I wasn't onstage, too! She yearned to be part of it all—not as a stumbling intruder, but as a friend.

"Hit a rough patch out on 220," Buddy said, laughing. "Old Cheryl grabbed me so hard she nearly choked my guts out, right, Cheryl?"

"I'm still shaking," Cheryl said, pulling a pack of cigarettes from her shirt pocket. She held it up to Rosalie. "Smoke?"

"No, thanks," Rosalie said politely. She watched Cheryl light her cigarette. She wondered how Tony and

Jill knew people like her and Buddy. They seemed so different.

Lisa jumped up from the floor, brushing at her skirt. "Look out, Buddy! You're spilling beer all over me."

Buddy laughed. "Open your mouth, I'll pour some right in." He grabbed Lisa's arm.

Maybe he's crazy or something, Rosalie thought. She tried to push her stool back, out of the way. She teetered awkwardly for a minute, and caught herself.

"Don't mind old Buddy," Tony said, looking at Rosalie while he stroked Jill's hair. "He's been my friend from way back—grade school, high school, all the way."

"All the way, that's me." Buddy sat down on the couch, almost on top of Jill. She was half his size. Rosalie thought he was awful. He was probably exactly what her mother meant when she talked about wild parties. But Jill and Tony weren't wild. They looked so happy and peaceful that Rosalie couldn't take her eyes off them.

"Do you go to Vandam High?" Ken, the man who had been there on moving day, bent toward her.

"Junior High," Rosalie said shyly. At least he must have thought she was older.

"So did I, way back when. Ever have Mr. Wade for science?"

"I have him now!" Rosalie said, eagerly. "Isn't he neat? I really love him!" Embarrassed by her enthusiasm, she took another swallow of Coke. He'd think she was a dope.

But Ken answered, "Really," as though she'd said something significant.

Lisa turned to Rosalie. "Ken and I went to Vandam, too. We graduated in Seventy-two, before they built the addition."

Rosalie was surprised. "Seventy-two!" She would only have been eight or nine in 1972.

Lisa laughed. "It wasn't really so long ago." She put her arm around Ken. "Ken was my high school sweetheart, right, Kenny?" Rosalie couldn't tell whether she was teasing. She couldn't imagine making jokes about something like that. The fragments of conversation around her were confusing. She wished her toe would stop hurting; it was hard to concentrate on anything else. She looked down at her white pants. They were brown at the knees where she'd fallen on them. Her thighs looked enormous. She put her hands down to cover them.

Jill jumped up and ran to the kitchen. She grabbed some hot pads and pulled at the oven door. "Hey, guys, I think the pizza's ready." The plastic handle came off in her hands and she tipped backward. "Damn!" she said, catching herself. "Now what?" she called to Tony. "The pizza's going to burn up in there."

Tony went to the stove, pushing the table aside to make room for the two of them. He grabbed a knife and pried the oven door open. "I can glue it back on," he said. "It didn't really break."

"Well, it didn't really work, either," Jill said tensely. "Look out—move back!" She pulled the pizza from the oven, grimacing, and set the pan on the sink.

Rosalie wished she could go and help, but she knew she could never stand up and walk across the room in front of everyone. Besides, there wouldn't be room for her in the small kitchen. Self-consciousness flooded over her again. She wondered whether she was supposed to stay and eat pizza with everyone else, or whether Jill's serving the food was some kind of signal that she should go home. But how could she leave, without standing up and saying something? She shifted uncomfortably on the small stool.

Buddy yelled, "I hope you threw the works on—mushrooms, anchovies, sausage, garlic, everything. That's the way ole Buddy likes it."

"Ech, anchovies!" Jill said. "Not on my pizza."

Buddy jumped up, grabbing Cheryl. "Come on, woman, we're getting out of here. No anchovies on the pizza!"

Cheryl stepped back, bumping into Rosalie's toe. Rosalie had to work to keep from crying out.

Suddenly they were all crowding around the coffee table.

"Get me something to put under the pan, quick!" Jill called.

Buddy took a book from the shelf behind him. *"Principles of Case Work*—that looks thick enough to hold a pizza."

"Hey, no!" Jill shouted. "That's my good book, Buddy. I don't want pizza sauce all over it. Get me a towel or something."

At this, Rosalie got up. She went to the kitchen and pulled a dish towel off the rack. Jill smiled at her gratefully.

"Excuse me," Rosalie said, putting the towel on the table. Then she went back to her stool.

Tony said, "Jill's going to solve the world's problems in one semester, with that book."

Jill looked up at him quickly. Rosalie wondered if he was teasing.

"Well, don't come case-working around me," Buddy said. "I know those types. You better watch out, you'll turn into one of them, nosy and self-righteous."

"Hey!" Jill said, obviously hurt. She set the pizza on the coffee table. "Don't talk like that!"

Rosalie wanted to comfort her. But Tony put his arm around Jill protectively. "Don't mind Buddy; he just wants to rile you up a little."

Jill smiled.

Now everyone began to pull at the pizza except Rosalie, who sat fixed and embarrassed on her stool, and Tony and Jill, who stood under the lamp. Tony stroked Jill's shoulder and her head leaned against his chest. Rosalie thought she had never seen anything so romantic.

"The biggest piece!" Buddy yelled, while melting cheese dripped from his slice. "That's what I go for, eh, Cheryl?"

Cheryl snickered.

Tony and Jill moved apart.

"Come on, Rosalie," Tony said, noticing her. "Come on. Have some pizza."

Ken moved aside to make room for her on the floor. Rosalie sat down awkwardly, trying not to bump into him or the table. She pulled her legs up under her as far as she could. She knew that she would be terribly uncomfortable in this position, but she was too shy to shift. So she sat where she was, reaching out for a slice of pizza and setting it down on a napkin in front of her. It smelled wonderful. She wished she could eat pizza and not get fat, like Jill and Lisa. Cautiously, so she wouldn't drip cheese onto her chin, she took a small bite, keeping her elbow down so she wouldn't bump Ken. She wondered if they all minded her being there.

But nobody seemed to be paying attention to her. They were all busy eating. Tony put on a new record and the music started up again, cheery and bright. Despite her cramped position, Rosalie relaxed for the first time since she'd come into the trailer. It's like I'm just one of the people at the party, she thought.

"The pizza's good," she told Jill.

"Thanks. I made it—you know, not from a mix or anything. From scratch."

"She has to do everything the hard way, my wife," Tony said, grinning at Jill.

Rosalie loved the way he said "my wife."

"It's great," Ken said. "If I could find somebody to make me pizza like this, I'd get married too."

Rosalie wondered if she would ever feel grown-up enough to joke around like that about something as important as getting married. She doubted it. After all, she didn't even like her mother or Maxine to tease her about Ed.

Ken moved a bit, and Rosalie carefully shifted her legs into the space he'd left. She leaned back against the board-and-brick bookcase. The music played on, conversation rose and fell around her, smoke spiraled wispily toward the wall lamps. Jill smiled at Tony. Even Buddy, with Cheryl leaning against his knees, seemed calm.

I'm here! Rosalie thought. It's really me, eating pizza with grown people at a party. She pushed her hair back from her face in what she hoped was an easy, graceful gesture. Looking up, she caught Tony's eye. He smiled at her. She thought he was probably the handsomest man she had ever seen. And Jill the cutest woman. And here she was in their trailer!

Then, just when things were starting to go right, she heard the call.

"Rosalie? Rosalie!"

Rosalie jumped up awkwardly, bumping into the table. The pizza pan clattered. Rosalie stepped back onto Cheryl's ash tray.

"Oh, I'm sorry!" She bent down and tried to retrieve the scattered butts.

"Rosalie!"

The call came right through the window. Don't let her come in! Rosalie thought wildly.

"That's my mom," she said to Jill. "I have to go." She stumbled toward the door, opened it, and called out. "I'm here. I'm coming."

They were all staring at her. Rosalie searched for Jill's face.

"Thanks for the party," she said, finding it. "I had a very good time. I really love your place." She tried to look at all the rest of them. "It was very nice to meet you," she blurted, and ran out.

The night air smelled fresh and cool.

Rita stood at the foot of the steps, clutching her pocketbook. The music was loud, even with the door closed. Rosalie could hear laughter over it. She wondered if they were laughing at her.

"I just went over for a couple of minutes," she began, limping down the steps.

Without a word, Rita turned toward the house.

Rosalie followed her through the lilacs and into the kitchen.

Then Rita let go.

"I've been out of my mind, looking for you! How do you think I felt, coming home and the house wide open and nobody there?" She put her hand to her chest. "I was worried sick, Rosalie."

"I'm sorry—"

"Sorry!" Rita snorted. "Is that all you can say, just, you're sorry? All the lights on, the door open so anybody could walk right in here, no note or anything—what kind of way is that to treat your mother? I'm surprised at you, Rosalie. Honest I am. Scaring me half to death. Thank God for that awful music. I finally put two and two together, figured out you had to be over there—"

Rosalie stood silently behind a chair.

"Don't you have anything to say for yourself?"

"No—just, I'm really sorry I worried you, Mom. Honest."

Rita looked at her suspiciously. "What were you doing, anyway, hanging around back there?"

"See, I saw people going in the trailer and I just went out to look—"

"You were practically spying, that's what you were doing. You ought to be ashamed. *I'm* ashamed. I don't know what those people will think of us. Look at you— your hair a mess, filthy pants. I can't stand those baggy pants anyway, they make you look so fat. And your shirt. Didn't I tell you nine dollars was too much to pay for a T-shirt? Now look at it, with that hole smack in the middle. . . ."

Rita put her head down on her arms, turning her face from Rosalie. "And me throwing my money away at that damn Bingo like some millionaire, just because for once in my life I got a couple dollars extra tips. I should have saved that five dollars I gave you for myself. I go around in the same old clothes so you can have nice things, and then, look at you!"

She raised her head and threw her arm toward Rosalie in a gesture of helplessness. Except for ritual spanks, Rita had never struck her. To Rosalie this hopeless wave was worse than a blow. She moved to touch her mother, but Rita pulled away.

"Leave me alone. I don't wanna talk about it any more right now. Just let me be."

Rosalie went to bed overwhelmed by her mother's anger and her own feeling of shame. Lying in bed with her arms curled tightly across her chest, she went over and over the horrible fall in the lilacs. Jill must have known she was spying. She probably just asked her in out of pity. Rosalie tossed in bed, unable to squelch the memory of how she had sat on that awful stool, towering above everyone. She was so big and awkward and young and out of place! How could she have gone in at all? Too late, she imagined herself lightly refusing Jill's offer of help and limping with dignity back to her house. Oh, why hadn't she come home? What could she possibly say to her mother in the morning? And how would she ever be able to face Tony and Jill again?

Miserable, she tossed in her bed until she fell asleep.

9

The next morning, the trailer—so clearly, closely *there* outside the window—intruded into the kitchen as Rosalie and Rita ate a silent breakfast.

Both of them tensed as a clatter of cans dropping into a metal garbage can came from the yard next door. Rita glanced up, muttering sourly about people getting drunk. Rosalie didn't answer.

"I suppose you think it's hot stuff, drinking and carrying on all hours of the night," Rita shot out. "Well, listen here, Miss Rosalie Hudnecker. You just let me catch you one time with alcohol on your breath and I swear you won't go out of this house nights for the next six months."

"Mom, all I had over there was a Coke. Honest! That's all most of them had."

"Never mind, I saw those cases of beer go in. It's gonna get drunk up sometime. I'm just telling you to stay out of it."

Rosalie sighed. She wished she could explain to Rita how wonderful Tony and Jill were. But it didn't matter. They'd never want her to come over again, after last night. After she'd made such a fool of herself, in front of their friends. If only, she said to herself for the hundredth time. If only I hadn't spoiled everything. She thought of the dream in which the three of them were so close. Now it would never come true.

"Look at this, will you," Rita said in a different tone, studying an article in *Sunday Parade*. "A whole darned article about chairs, and not a single one of them looks like it could hold a person up, the little spindly things." She read out a caption. " 'Two hundred dollars for this authentic reproduction of an early American kitchen chair.' " She sat back, looked around the kitchen, and snorted. "They oughta come to this place. I could tell them plenty about old American chairs, with the slats loose, too. Maybe that makes them more valuable."

Rosalie smiled. She wondered what Jill would think of their kitchen chairs—and their kitchen. The familiar room, which Rosalie had always taken for granted, looked plain and harsh after the trailer's soft glow.

She glanced up just as Tony and Jill walked up Mrs. Cree's steps, holding hands. They looked so far away! She could hardly believe she had been right in their house last night. Trying not to attract Rita's attention, she watched them talking through Mrs. Cree's kitchen door. After a few minutes, the Judsons went back to the trailer. Jill was almost hopping to keep up with Tony's long stride. Rosalie sat back in her chair, but stiffened up as Mrs. Cree came out of her house, her apron strings flapping about her thin legs. She was heading straight for the Hudneckers!

Rita looked up from her paper just as Mrs. Cree climbed up their back steps and pushed the doorbell hard, hanging on to it as though it was they who were deaf and not her.

"Look who's here! There goes my Sunday peace and quiet, such at it is," Rita grumbled, going to the door.

Mrs. Cree walked right in and sat down. "Thought I'd come over and tell you how things are working out over to the trailer," she began.

Rita's mouth set in a tight line.

"A real nice young couple they are, it seems like," Mrs.

Cree went on. "Course, it does take some getting used to, the yard cut smack in half and that car of theirs going in and out all the time. But it's a good investment, like the lawyer said. You ought to consider it, Rita. Cut down your apple tree, it never fruits anyhow, and you'd have a nice space for a trailer right there, and a steady income against your old age. They say the demand for mobile homes is getting bigger all the time. All the young folks want to live in one of 'em."

Rosalie knew that Rita would be furious at Mrs. Cree's implication that they were in the same boat. Rita had watched Mrs. Cree slip slowly into crotchety deafness over the years. More than once she had worried out loud to Maxine and Rosalie that she might grow old and cranky like Mrs. Cree. "So deaf that nobody's gonna put up with me," she'd said.

But now she was angry. "I'm not about to cut that apple tree down, thank you," she said, "and have some strangers sitting right on top of me in my back yard. The trailer's bad enough," she added in a low voice that Mrs. Cree wouldn't pick up.

"You want what?" Mrs. Cree fumbled with her hearing aid.

"Not gonna cut down the tree!" Rita yelled.

"Well, sure, hold out while you can, long as you can afford to," Mrs. Cree said in the voice of experience. "Just remember what I told you, you couldn't find a better investment to keep you out of the old folks' home."

Exasperated, Rita shouted, "I'm not thinking about *that* yet!"

"That's just the trouble," said Mrs. Cree complacently. "People don't plan ahead, think about the future, that's why they get in trouble later on."

"How long did they rent for?" Rosalie asked, as casually as she could, as though she were just being polite.

"What?"

"The Judsons. How long are they staying?" She was afraid her words would carry over to the trailer if she yelled any louder.

"Yes, college students, a nice type of renter." Mrs. Cree paused to let the question sink in. Then she answered it. "Took the trailer for three months, spring and summer term. Or what's left of the spring. It started up a week before they even moved in. That's what comes of me believing all those promises the tree man gave me. But I'd rent it to them again in the fall, if they asked. Nice, agreeable people. None of your common riffraff."

She paused and sat back in her chair. Then she came out with what Rosalie and her mother recognized as the reason for her visit.

"Now, they just stopped by the house to ask me for a shovel and a rake so they could start digging up a little garden in front of their place. My shovel handle's broke, so I told them, I said, maybe you want to go over to the Hudneckers'. It'd give you a nice chance to get acquainted, I said. I told them about you, Rosalie. I said, there's a girl you want to get to know. But Tony said you already got acquainted. Said you came to a little party they threw last night. Not that they're the loud, partying kind," she added, an eye on Rita. "I didn't hear a sound from there last night."

After Mrs. Cree left, Rita let go. "I'm not gonna let Mrs. Cree sic those people on us for everything they need. Just because she's too cheap to buy anything when she thinks she can borrow it. I don't intend to start lending out our things to those people, Rosalie, even if they should be nervy enough to come here asking me. Let them find out, if they want to play house, the money it takes just to keep a place running." She sighed and began to fold up the paper.

"If I don't sit right down and take care of the seams in my uniform," she said, "it's gonna be good-bye, uniform. The new lot they got in at Mastersons' costs sixteen ninety-eight, would you believe it? Doreen bought one last week, and it's not a bit better made than the old ones." She leaned against the sink. "Honestly, sometimes it just seems like *everything*'s gone sky-high. Food, clothes, you name it."

"Let me get your sewing basket," Rosalie said, feeling sorry for her mother. "Do you want the whole basket, or just a needle and thread?"

"Might as well bring it all down—and give me that T-shirt of yours while you're at it. Let's see what I can do with the hole." She smiled at Rosalie as though she wanted the tension between them to disappear.

"Thanks, Mom." Rosalie went upstairs and looked out her bedroom window to see whether Jill and Tony might be coming over. But there was no sight of them. If only Mrs. Cree hadn't made things worse, she thought bitterly. She wished she would never have to face Tony or Jill again. At the same time, the thought of not seeing them—of never again sitting in that small, cozy room with the yellow lights glowing—was almost more painful than she could bear. She wondered if the Judsons had even thought of her since last night. If they did, they probably just laughed about her. She didn't mean a thing to them, she told herself. And yet she didn't know how she could possibly give them up.

Rosalie heard a knock downstairs at the kitchen door. Listening warily from the hall, she made out Jill's voice and then her mother's. They talked briefly. Then Jill laughed awkwardly, and the door slammed shut.

Rosalie carried the sewing basket downstairs.

"I guess I nipped that business in the bud," Rita said with satisfaction. "She seems like a nice enough little girl, polite as can be. But once that kind of thing starts up, borrowing this, borrowing that, there won't be any end to it. Anyway, I don't know where our shovel is and that's the truth, just like I told her."

Rosalie hoped her mother hadn't said anything to hurt Jill's feelings. That would be awful! She stopped herself from telling Rita that the shovel was in the garage, behind Joe Pat's old tires. Maybe she could use the shovel for an excuse to go back over to the trailer. If she had the nerve to face them again. But it would be good to take them something they needed. She wondered how she could go there without Rita finding out.

Suddenly, without warning, Maxine walked in, bursting with enthusiasm.

"What kind of way is that to spend a beautiful spring Sunday?" She looked at Rita's sewing basket. "For heaven's sake, Rita. You ought to be ashamed of yourself, sitting inside sewing on a beautiful day like this." She pulled the uniform out of Rita's hands and put it on the kitchen table.

"Believe it or not, Charlie's out front in the car. We're going over to his brother's place to see the new patio furniture they got. Gonna pick up some steak at the Park 'n' Shop and have a barbecue in their back yard." She paused to hug Rosalie. "How's it going, hon? How about coming along with your mom, bring a ray of sunshine to us old folks?"

"Who says *I'm* coming?" Rita demanded. But she folded up her uniform and put it on top of the sewing basket. For the first time that day she was really smiling.

"Don't argue. You don't have to change. Just grab a

sweater in case it turns chilly. Come on. If you don't hurry up, Charlie's gonna change his mind and head straight back home. Believe me, it's not easy to get that man off the couch and over to visit his relations."

In two minutes Rita and Maxine were gone.

Rosalie knew that Maxine and Charlie would hear the whole story of the party in the trailer, along with Mrs. Cree's morning visit and Jill's request for the shovel. She hated to think about it.

But now, she realized, she was free. She could go over to Tony and Jill's and lend them the shovel. She could apologize for how she had acted the night before. Maybe she could sit in the trailer with them and have a real visit.

Still, Rosalie hesitated. It was awful to want to do something so badly and yet be afraid to do it. It felt like last night, all over again. At the thought of that uncomfortable evening, Rosalie almost changed her mind.

But how was she going to get close to them if she didn't make an effort? Rosalie went upstairs and washed her face. Then she picked up her hairbrush and brushed her hair with hard, angry strokes.

She looked at herself in the mirror. She couldn't decide whether she looked any different. She wished she looked older and more sophisticated—like the kind of person who had older friends. But it seemed as though only the same Rosalie, heavy and childish, her frizzy hair a wild mass, looked back at her. Rosalie grabbed the hairbrush hard and swatted it down. Then she ran out to the garage and, rummaging behind the pile of dusty tires, pulled the shovel out.

This won't be like the party, she thought. I won't be busting in on them; I'll be taking them something they want. This time, they'll really be glad to see me.

10

As Rosalie pushed the shovel through the lilacs, she had a sudden change of heart. But it was too late to back out now; Tony or Jill might have seen her from the window. So she straightened up, and holding the shovel in front of her like a spear, walked straight to the trailer steps. She climbed up and knocked on the door.

There was a small flurry and scuffling inside. Immediately, Rosalie regretted being there. What if they had been kissing?

"Just a second," Jill called. Then she opened the door. She stared at Rosalie and the shovel for a minute, as though trying to understand. Then she smiled.

"Oh, hi. You *found* it. That's surely nice of you, to bring it over."

"That's O.K." Rosalie stood stiffly on the doorstep.

"Tony, guess what?" Jill called. "Rosalie brought their shovel over."

There was a grunt from the back of the trailer.

"Well," Jill said brightly. "Aren't you going to come in and pay a little visit, now you're here?"

Rosalie didn't know what to do. Did Jill mean it, or was that just her polite, southern way of talking?

Jill smiled. "Come on."

"Well, thanks. Just for a minute. I have to get back—" Still holding the shovel, Rosalie followed Jill inside.

It looked different in the daylight.

The striped spread had slipped off the couch, revealing

the tan plastic cover beneath it. The coffee table was piled with ash trays and cups and scraps of pizza crust. Two straight chairs blocked the way into the kitchen, where the counters were covered with dirty glasses and plates. The stool on which Rosalie had sat so uncomfortably the night before lay on its side by the bookcase. At the sight of it, Rosalie remembered how awkward and out of place she had felt last night. Why did I ever come back? she thought. But she knew she would be ready to endure any embarrassment, just to be close to Jill and Tony in this special place. She looked around. Sunlight glowed through the yellow curtains and lit up the leaves of the plant in the corner. Even messed up like this, the trailer was beautiful.

"Sit down," Jill said. She took the shovel and set it by the door.

Rosalie sat on the edge of the couch. From here she could see to the far end of the trailer, where a door stood open, showing the corner of an unmade bed with sheets and blankets on the floor. Tony came out of this room, smoothing his beard and hair with his fingers.

"Hello, Rosalie. I guess you've spoiled my excuse for not working."

She wasn't sure whether he was kidding or not. But then he smiled at her. He has such a nice smile, she thought.

"Give me a minute, anyway, to sit down with you beautiful women." He sat down opposite Rosalie on the couch.

Rosalie was thrilled to be included in his teasing. It's so different, she thought, being here alone with the two of them. It's so homey. The disarray just made it seem more real. After all, she told herself, in real life there have to be dirty dishes.

"We didn't get around to cleaning up yet, we slept so late," Jill explained. "Would you believe, Cheryl and Buddy stayed till three this morning?"

"That's old Buddy for you," Tony said. "Doesn't know when to quit." He laughed.

"Well, I would have thought Cheryl would say something," Jill said.

"Cheryl wasn't dying to go out and ride thirty miles on the back of a bike."

Jill jumped up. "I never offered you something, Rosalie. How about a Coke?" She went to the kitchen and squatted in front of the small refrigerator, searching the shelves. "Beer! It seems like that's all there is in here, is beer."

"Best thing for a hangover," Tony said, winking at Rosalie.

Jill looked up. "Tony! You know that neither Rosalie nor I have a hangover, and I certainly hope you don't either." She made a face and slammed the refrigerator door shut. "How about a cup of coffee, Rosalie? We've got plenty of instant, if you don't mind instant."

"Sure, if it isn't any trouble," Rosalie said. She hated coffee, but she didn't want to say so. Everybody but kids liked it.

Jill hunted among the stacked dishes. "There must be some cups here somewhere." Her hand brushed against a glass on the edge of the counter. It fell, shattering onto the floor.

"Now you've done it!" Tony picked up the shovel. "I'm getting out of here." He pretended to sneak out the door.

Rosalie jumped down on her knees to search for glass on the floor. She picked up some big pieces and pushed them carefully into the overflowing trash basket.

"My mom says, after you get all the big pieces, take the wet paper towel and go over the floor to get the little splinters up."

"That's just the same thing my mom says!" Jill smiled at her. She handed Rosalie a wet towel and they went over the linoleum together, dabbing at the thin shreds of glass. Rosalie noticed enviously how cute Jill looked in her jeans and yellow shirt, with her dark hair falling over her eyes. Rosalie felt awkward squatting down like this. She hoped Tony wouldn't come in and see how big she looked, down on the floor next to Jill.

Jill straightened up. "I'm certainly not entertaining you very well." She threw her towel away. "Come on, now, Rosalie. Quit. I'm sure we got it all. Let me make us some coffee."

Rosalie didn't want the good feeling of working with Jill to end. "Couldn't I help you with the dishes?"

"Oh, no. I wouldn't want you to do that," Jill said, not very firmly.

"I'd like it though," Rosalie insisted. She would be happy to do their dishes, scrub their floors—anything, she thought, just to have a reason for being here with them. And if they saw how helpful she could be, maybe they would ask her over, again and again, and she would become almost like—well, like one of them.

They could hear the shovel clinking against the cement base of the trailer. It pleased Rosalie to think of them all at work, Tony outside and Jill and herself in here. Almost like a family.

"Please, let's," she pressed.

"Well—" Jill frowned at the counter top. "If you really want to. It would be a relief to get this mess cleaned up. The trailer's so small, it makes you feel awful when things are every which way." She reached under the sink for a plastic dishpan and began to run water into it.

As she wiped each glass carefully, Rosalie felt a surge of happiness. It was fun to put things away in their places inside the little trailer cupboards. It was different from doing dishes at home, where the cups were chipped and the forks and spoons were stained. Jill's dishes all matched. They were heavy, mustard-yellow pottery. Her spoons and forks were shiny stainless steel. Even the dish towel, covered with a delicate print of green herbs, was pretty. The dish towels at home were like rags.

"Your things are so nice," Rosalie said. "I just love your dishes."

"Oh, thanks. We chose them together, before we got married. It was fun, picking everything out."

Rosalie thought of Joe Pat's wedding dishes. They were white, with a red-and-green plaid design. She had thought they were nice when they were displayed on a lace tablecloth at Joanne's house before the wedding. Now they seemed dull and old-fashioned.

"It must be fun to fix up a house just the way you want it," she said.

"Oh, I love it," Jill said. "Not that I'd want to live in a trailer forever—"

"But it's so wonderful in here!" Rosalie said.

Tony came in the door, wiping his face on his shirt sleeve. "That's hot work."

He reached across Jill and took a glass from the cupboard. He ran water into it and gulped it down. Then he smiled at Rosalie. "Glad to see the womenfolk working."

Rosalie glowed.

Jill made a wry face. "Want to trade?"

"No, thanks!" Tony laughed and went back out.

"Look at all that dirt he tracked in here," Jill said. "I

never did know any one person who could make so much mess so fast."

Rosalie loved her fond tone. She looked out the window where Tony was digging, his shirt plastered to his body. "What are you going to plant out there?"

"Petunias, like my mother always had back home. You know those dark blue ones? And geraniums. I guess I'm a little bit homesick for flowers. We used to have them everywhere. Mom started working in the garden the minute frost was over. It seems like you have to wait a long time for that, up North."

"How come you moved?"

"See, my dad works for J. C. Penney and he got transferred last year." She sighed. "Mom felt real bad about it, leaving all her family. And my sister. It was the worst for her. She was right in the middle of high school. She cried for weeks." Jill looked thoughtfully at Rosalie. "You sort of remind me of her."

"I do?" Rosalie couldn't see how a sister of Jill's would be big.

"You have those same kind of eyes, big and so dark they look like they're black. I always thought it was no fair that Bobbie Jean had eyes like that and mine were so wishy-washy."

"I think you have nice eyes," Rosalie said sincerely. "I just love how you look!" she blurted out. "I wish I was little and pretty like you."

Like most people who are used to compliments, Jill didn't act surprised. "To tell the truth," she said, "I never thought I'd catch Tony. He's crazy about tall girls. His last girl friend was six feet tall, with heels on."

Rosalie had never before thought that anyone—any man—would actually have such a preference. She resolved to stand very straight when Tony was around.

"Like that Lisa, last night," Jill said.

Rosalie's spirits sank. Lisa was tall, but she was thin. "Does she go to Carpenter Community too?"

"Yeah. Lisa and Ken and Bill. Tony met them in some class. I don't really know them that well." She emptied the dishpan, wiped it dry, and put it away. "I don't know why they make these cupboards so small," she complained. "And give you such a little tiny refrigerator. And look at that dinette set—you can put a cloth on the table, but I don't see any way to cover up the chairs."

Rosalie was surprised. She had been wishing they had a nice set like Jill's at home.

Jill pulled her arm. "Want to see the worst of all? Come and look at the bathroom."

She threw open the bathroom door. Rosalie peered in. She didn't know what Jill meant. The bathroom looked so nice, with Jill's bottles and jars and lipsticks laid out on the shelf above the basin, and Tony's shaving things on the basin itself. A small blue nylon nightgown hung on the wall beside a pair of striped pajamas. Rosalie blushed. It was like peeking at Jill and Tony's private life. She thought the bathroom was wonderful, like the rest of the trailer. There were even cute little dogs on the shower curtain.

"I mean, look at those awful *dogs*," Jill said in disgust.

Rosalie was glad she hadn't said anything. "I just love your whole place," she confided. "I think it's the cutest little house I ever saw."

The shovel clattered against the wall outside. Jill and Rosalie went to the kitchen window and looked out. Tony had dug up a small plot the width of the trailer. The earth looked dry and powdery. Jill clapped her hands at Tony through the window.

Tony grinned, bowed, and came inside.

"Thanks, hon," Jill said. Right in front of Rosalie she walked over and hugged him. Her head came only up to his chest. Over it, Tony smiled at Rosalie.

"I guess I earned my ball game for sure. Paid my dues for this day."

"Oh, Tony," Jill said right away. "You know Rosalie and I don't want to see some old ball game."

"I ought to go," Rosalie said quickly. She didn't want to get caught here if they were going to have an argument.

"I thought we were going to have a nice quiet conversation." Jill looked at Tony. "But who can hear themselves think with that thing turned way up?"

Tony's eyes were on the set.

Rosalie hated to go. But she went to the door. "I'll take the shovel back home if you're finished. Just ask, if you need it again. But you better ask *me*, though," she said quickly. "Mom never can find it."

"Wait," Jill said. "Listen, Rosalie—why don't you come over for dinner some night next week? I'll make you some real southern fried chicken." She sounded as though she really meant it.

Rosalie was flattered. A real invitation! She waited to see if Tony would urge her to come too. But he was absorbed in the television screen.

Jill walked in front of it to block his view. "Tony! Be polite, at least. What about next Thursday, for Rosalie to come over? We get home about five thirty on Thursdays. We could eat at six thirty."

"Sure," Tony said. "If Rosalie doesn't mind burned chicken."

"Tony!" Jill laughed.

Rosalie realized he was just kidding. "Thanks, I'd love to come," she said sincerely.

Tony pulled Jill down beside him on the couch. He

smiled over at Rosalie. "See you Thursday."

Jill kicked off her shoes, pulled her feet up under her, and leaned back against Tony. "Thanks for bringing the shovel over, Rosalie. And for helping me clean up. That was real nice of you."

They seemed to be waiting for her to go. Rosalie let herself out of the trailer and stood at the top of the steps, looking over at her bedroom window. It seemed amazing that she was here instead of in there, watching. She walked down the steps, already imagining herself back in the trailer, sitting at the little table eating supper with Tony and Jill. Dinner, she corrected herself. That's what Jill had called it. It seemed as though a lot of wonderful things were beginning to happen. Wait till I tell Judy, she thought. About the party, and this afternoon, and about the invitation. She wished Tony and Jill hadn't been sort of arguing when Judy saw them yesterday. After all, everybody argued sometimes. Joe Pat and Joanne, even. Anyway, she was sure Judy would be impressed when she heard about the party.

Rosalie put the shovel back in the garage, hoping that neither Tony or Jill would thank her mother for it. She wondered how to raise the subject of the dinner invitation. I'll wait a couple of days, she told herself.

She was going up the steps when Charlie's big station wagon pulled into the driveway. Maxine got out first, then Rita, both of them laughing.

Rosalie waved.

"Hey, there, Rosie! Whaddya trying to do, rush inside and ignore me?" Charlie leaned out of his window. "I havent seen you for a month of Sundays."

His round, kind face always made Rosalie feel good. "Hi, Charlie. You coming in?"

"Nope, we've been gallivanting around long enough.

It's time to go home and put our feet up," he said cheerfully.

"O.K., but hold it just one minute," Maxine said, "till I give the kid a kiss."

She ran up the steps and grabbed Rosalie close, smacking her on the cheek. As usual, she smelled like the shop. Maxine did her own hair as carefully as the customers' and held it in place with generous amounts of the hair spray she bought at wholesale.

"What've you been doing with yourself, Rosie?" she asked. "Out with your friends?"

"No, just hanging around," Rosalie said, feeling guilty. Maxine, like Rita, loved to hear about things she did with her friends. Stories about school dances or dates for the movies or slumber parties—all those childish things. Rosalie couldn't explain how unimportant stuff like that seemed now. Now that she had new, grown friends, with their own place.

"Probably talking on the phone," Rita teased comfortably. "Using up all our extra message units, the minute my back's turned."

Maxine got back into the car, and Charlie backed it down the driveway.

"Thanks!" Rita waved after them. "I had a real nice time!" She looked over toward the trailer. "I see they got their flower bed dug up over there, after all. Wonder where they got hold of a shovel. Mr. Garrity must have lent them his."

Rosalie didn't answer. It was going to be hard to explain things to her mother, now that she was getting close to Tony and Jill. And she didn't want to have to explain. She hoped her mother wouldn't start prying or nagging at her about it. The trailer was so special. She wanted to keep her feelings about it to herself.

11

"What's got into you, spring fever?"

Rita stood by the door with her car keys and addressed Rosalie's back. "You'd better get a move on, instead of standing there mooning out the window. You're gonna be late for school."

Rosalie turned around. "I hate school!"

"What kind of talk is that? For somebody who just made all that fuss about the academic course. I'm glad Mrs. Johnson can't hear you now. She'd scratch you right off that list of hers."

"They treat you like such a baby."

Rita shook her keys. "They'd treat you like an adult if you'd act like one, take a positive attitude." She looked sharply at Rosalie. "You oughta go right back upstairs and brush that hair of yours down. Give it a good hundred strokes. I'm ashamed for anyone to think I can't even get my daughter to keep her hair decent. If you'd just let me or Maxine give you some nice short cut—"

"All right!" Suddenly Rosalie was furious. "If it'll make you stop nagging at me all the time, I *will*. I'll get it all cut off, if that's what you want. I'll get a crew cut, for God's sake!"

"Rosalie!"

"Leave me alone," Rosalie shouted. "Just leave me alone!" She was instantly frightened by the look on her mother's face.

"I swear I don't know what's the matter with you these

days," Rita began, as though she had been waiting to say it. She pulled out a chair and sat down heavily. "It seems like all you do is mope around the house, complaining. And not lifting a finger unless I get after you. Look at this floor. It hasn't been mopped in about two weeks. I thought you might think of doing it yesterday when I went out, but I should've known better. Look at the yard. It hasn't been touched all spring. Mr. Garrity's mowed his yard three, four times already. This place could go to the dogs, for all you care about it." She paused, and her tone changed. "You having some kind of trouble with Ed?"

"No, I'm not having some kind of trouble with Ed," Rosalie said angrily.

"What's the matter, then, hon? What's got into you?"

"Nothing's the matter. It's just, I don't know, I wish —" Rosalie searched for something tangible. "I wish it looked nicer in here. Look at how food's stuck in that crack in the table. It's disgusting. Why can't we ever have a tablecloth?"

Now Rita was furious. "That kind of *talk's* disgusting, Rosalie. I don't see you getting the can of Ajax out and scrubbing the table, put a little elbow grease to it. All you think of is covering up the dirt with some cloth. And what do you mean, you wish it looked nicer? You want this house in *House and Garden*? All I ask is for it to be clean and decent. Not that I wouldn't like a brand-new fancy dinette set, or a living-room rug that wasn't worn right down to the bare. The day I have money for stuff like that, that's what I'll call nicer. But how do you think I can save up for nice things when the price of just food is so high I feel sick every time I get in the checkout line?"

"Mom, I didn't mean it how it sounded. I'm sorry."

Rita went to the door. "You ought to be sorry. Aggravating me like this first thing in the morning." With her hand on the knob, she looked pleadingly at Rosalie.

"What's wrong, hon? It seems like we're at each other like cats and dogs all the time these days. If you'd just show a little concern. . . ."

"I don't know." Rosalie couldn't answer. "I don't mean—"

"If I stand here another minute I'm gonna be late." Rita's voice rose. "You just take a look around when you get home from school today and see what you can find to do that's useful."

"I have to go to the Carlsons today, Mom. I promised."

"I wish you'd promise your own mother some help." Rita started out. "You can tell Mrs. Carlson she's paying you just about half what you deserve. I don't want you working for slave wages over there in that fancy house of hers."

She ran down the steps and got into the car, slamming the door after her. The motor started up jumpily. Rita backed out in an angry screech of tires.

Rosalie was exhausted. Her breakfast orange juice sat acidly in her stomach. Shouting at her mother had brought a kind of relief, but she knew it would make her feel guilty all day. Trembling, she wet a dishcloth and wiped off the table, scrubbing hard at the crack in the mottled gray plastic top. That crack had been there since she could remember. Why did she have to pick this morning to complain about it?

Automatically, she looked out the window.

Jill came out of the trailer in a navy blue sweater that Rosalie hadn't seen before. She bent to look at the newly turned ground. Tony came out with his books and stood beside her. Rosalie could hardly bear the sight of their casual closeness. They seemed so distant, and so free.

Tony opened the car door, folded the front seat down, and threw his books in back. Then he got into the driver's seat, turned the engine over, and honked. Jill straightened up and ran to the other side of the car. Rosalie wondered if Jill knew how to drive. She never seemed to do it.

Opening her door, Jill looked past it and straight at the window where Rosalie stood. Seeing Rosalie there, she waved brightly.

Embarrassed to be caught staring, Rosalie jumped back, but it was too late. So she waved at Jill, trying to appear casual.

Jill didn't see the wave. She got into the car and bent toward Tony as they drove out. Rosalie felt queerly disappointed. Jill might have been waving at just anyone.

It's going to be different Thursday, she promised herself. On Thursday we'll really talk. The three of us. She pictured herself on their couch, telling Jill and Tony some funny story. She wondered what she should wear.

She went upstairs to her closet and pushed hopefully through her clothes, but only the familiar row of shirts and pants hung limply in front of her. She yearned for something new, something she would look really good in. All the clothes she owned made her look thick in the waist or fat in the stomach. It was so depressing to be fat! People like Jill or Judy would never understand. If only I was as thin as they are, she thought bitterly.

She turned to the mirror and stared at herself, looking straight at her heavy body in the large jeans and flapping shirt. I'm going to do it, she thought suddenly. I'm going to go on a diet and get thin. Really and truly. She wondered if she might even lose a pound or two before Thursday. That would be so wonderful!

Rosalie brushed her hair, thinking of her mother's complaints. She held a chunk of it back to see how it would look if it were short. Maybe it would be good. But she wasn't ready to try it yet. Anyway, she couldn't go to the trailer Thursday with a new haircut. They'd just think they had to say they liked it. Maybe, if the diet worked out, she could think about it.

She went downstairs, took an orange and a banana from the fruit bowl, and packed them into a paper bag for her lunch. There was a loaf of bread on the counter; just looking at it made her hungry. It wasn't going to be easy to hold out.

I can do it, she told herself. I can really do it. She pictured a new Rosalie, tall and thin, with a devastating new haircut, running lightly up the trailer steps for a visit with Tony and Jill. Or walking into the beauty shop while the customers whispered about Rita's stunning girl.

Rosalie looked at the clock, grabbed her bag of fruit, and ran outside. The trailer was still and empty in the morning sun. Rosalie could hardly remember how the woods used to look, and what it had been like to lie on soft pine needles staring up at the sky through sparkles of dust. In front of her house, she turned to look down Cedar Street at the Thruway ramp. High up on the cement ridge, small cars drove ceaselessly past Vandam on their way to someplace else. Rosalie wished she could go somewhere different, some place where she could be free and happy like Tony and Jill. Where you didn't have to argue with your mother, or rush to school every morning afraid of being late, or hurry through corridors all day at the command of shrill bells. She wondered how she would bear four whole more years of school. They said high school was fun, but you'd still be just a kid.

The warning bell was ringing as she reached the school door. At least she wouldn't be late. She ran to her locker and put her paper bag inside, already regretting the comfort of a decent lunch. But the sight of Amy Sebring at the next locker, with her tight shirt belted neatly into a thin skirt, strengthened her resolve. If she could only look like that!

"Hi, Rosalie," Amy said. "Have a good weekend?"

"Yeah, you?" Rosalie was sure she could impress Amy by talking about the trailer party, but she wasn't going to waste the story. She was saving it for Judy at lunch time.

Kids ran down the halls punching each other, laughing, trading taunts about weekend parties and dates. They act like babies, Rosalie thought in disgust. She remembered the sophisticated way Lisa and Ken and Bill had kidded each other Saturday night. Even Buddy was more interesting than the loud boys in this school.

Rosalie barely paid attention to what went on in social studies or English. She wondered what Jill and Tony were doing at Carpenter Community. They probably sat around in comfortable lounges, talking about classes. Or sat with their friends in coffee shops, or browsed through fascinating books in the library. Carpenter must be so different from this dumb school with its dull tan walls and boring green plastic chairs in rows.

By lunch time she was extravagantly hungry. She carried her bag of fruit to the table where her friends ate. No one was there yet. Rosalie decided to start with her orange and save the banana for a sort of desert. She poked her thumb into the orange and began to peel it. The sharp citrus scent contrasted oddly with the warm smell of stew from the cafeteria steam table. Rosalie sighed and bit into the orange.

Judy and Billy Kirchener came through the swinging doors. Except for being taller, Billy looked exactly as he had when they were in sixth grade together—round-faced and clownish. Rosalie hoped he wouldn't sit down with them. That would spoil her story.

Judy came to the table alone.

"Hi, Rosie." She plunked her lunch bag down on the table and looked at the orange. "You going on a diet?"

Rosalie made a face. If she said yes, everyone would make jokes about it and count her calories for her. Going on a diet was so public! She wished there was some way you could hide out till you got thin, like Mary Reddy, who was supposed to be visiting her aunt in Queens last year, though people whispered that she had really gone off to have a baby. Anyway, Mary Reddy came back thin.

"Not really," she said.

"Oh," said Judy, her mind on something else. "Where *were* you on Saturday night? I tried to call your house three different times, but no one answered. Billy and I decided to go to Pam's party and we wanted you to come with us."

"I thought you were going to the movies," Rosalie said, delaying her revelation.

"We went to the early show. Where *were* you, anyway?"

"Guess!"

"Come on, Rosie, how should I know?"

"At a party at the trailer!" Rosalie hoped she sounded cool. She watched eagerly for Judy's reaction.

Judy put her sandwich down. "You're kidding! How did you get invited?"

Rosalie had worked out this explanation. "See, I was just standing out in my yard and Jill saw me and she called and said I should come over because they were having a party. And I'm their neighbor."

"Wow! Who was there? Were they all older people?"

"Yeah." Rosalie was pleased with the effect she was

having. "You should have seen this one guy, Buddy—he came all the way from Strassberg on a motorcycle with his girl friend. He was awful! He was practically drunk and he kept saying these embarrassing things."

"So what's it like inside there?"

Rosalie despaired of explaining it adequately. "It's beautiful, honestly. She has all these pretty things— striped spreads and yellow dishes and plants. It's so cute and little—even the stove and refrigerator are little, like toys." She struggled to describe it right. "Jill and Tony are so neat together."

"Yeah, but remember when I was over? They sounded sort of angry."

"Anybody gets into arguments sometimes," Rosalie said quickly. "At the party, he had his arm around her all the time. She made pizza. I mean, she made it from scratch."

"That's neat. I wish I had someplace to go like that, instead of the same old parties with the same kids fooling around. And the same old onion dip."

Rosalie laughed. "And guess what—on Sunday, they wanted to borrow a shovel, so I took ours over. And I stayed a long time and talked. They even asked me for dinner Thursday!"

Judy was impressed. "Hey, you're really getting in with them." She drank up the last of her milk and crumpled the straw in her fingers. Then she looked expectantly at Rosalie. "Aren't you even going to ask how the play's going?"

Rosalie had completely forgotten it. "Oh, Judy—I'm sorry! How's it going?"

Judy turned serious. "Come and see for yourself. You better come if you still want to do makeup. It's only three weeks till performance." She looked straight at Rosalie.

"That is, unless you're too busy with your new friends."

"Judy!" Rosalie was ashamed to be thinking that she was. "I'll come," she said, hoping it wouldn't get in the way of a time in the trailer. "I want to see your costume and all. I meant to come before this. Well, anyway," she added lamely. "Isn't it neat about the Judsons? I never met people like them before. They're so neat. They do everything together, even the shopping."

Judy snorted. "What's so great about that? The Grand Union isn't exactly romantic. Hey—I got my job! Two to five, all summer. It'll probably be boring, but they pay two twenty-five an hour."

"I wish I could earn that much," Rosalie said. "Mrs. Carlson just gives me two. Mom's after me to ask for more when the new baby comes."

"You should."

"I don't know if I have the nerve."

Judy threw her crusts and her crumpled napkin into her paper bag. Rosalie watched her, trying not to think about how good the crusts would taste. Only a thin person could throw them away so easily. Rosalie gathered her orange rinds and the banana peel and put them into her own bag. One diet meal down, she thought, about five hundred to go.

The bell rang and they got up.

"Come to rehearsal soon," Judy said. "I want to show off to you, you know?"

"Yeah. And I really want to see you," Rosalie said, meaning it. Feeling hungry, she walked out of the lunch room.

12

At the end of the day, Rosalie grabbed her things from her locker and rushed out of school to avoid Ed. His house was near the Carlsons', and she usually walked over there with him. But she didn't want to see him today. She just didn't feel like telling him about Tony and Jill. It had been fun to show off about them to Judy, but it wouldn't be the same with Ed. He was so open about everything that he could make her feel like a little kid with a guilty secret. She knew that his matter-of-fact questions about the trailer might make her feel stupid. It was easier to avoid him than to try to tell him how she felt.

She hurried down the school walk. It was littered with candy wrappers, soda cans, and even people's jackets and sweaters. She dodged around the clumps of kids who stood challengingly in the middle of the walk and shouted taunts from the hoods of parked cars. On a nice day like this, everybody wanted to hang around outside. Rosalie hoped Mrs. Carlson wouldn't ask her to stay late. She was eager to get home and see what Tony and Jill were doing. Maybe they would come out to play Frisbee. Maybe they would ask her to join them.

"Rosalie!" Ed caught up with her on the sidewalk. "I didn't know you were walking this way today. Have a nice weekend?"

"Yeah." Rosalie was pleased to see him in spite of herself. She looked down at him over her books. He seemed shorter since the last time they'd been together.

"Did you go out?" She knew he wasn't prying. When he asked a question it was simply because he was interested.

"Yeah. I went to a party with the people in back, in the trailer." Rosalie decided it was easier not to lie. "You know, the guy you met the other night, Tony? And Jill. That's his wife." She watched for his reaction.

Ed was casual. "Yeah? What's it like back there?"

"It's O.K.," Rosalie said cautiously. "It's really pretty neat—" She stopped herself from saying he ought to see it.

"I'd like to see it," Ed said. "I can't believe you'd like it, after what that trailer did to the woods."

"Yeah, well—they fixed the trailer up real nice inside. And they're going to make a garden out front."

"Where? There isn't any room, I should think."

"Yes there is!" She didn't want Ed to be critical. What did he know about it? "It's going to be good. Jill's going to put in petunias and geraniums and everything." Rosalie wished he could see how nice it would be.

"Yeah, but still," Ed said. "It's just not the same anymore." Then he changed the subject. "My mom was really surprised when we gave her the sewing machine."

"What sewing machine?"

"You know. The one we got her for her birthday."

Rosalie had forgotten about it. "Oh. Did she like it?"

"Sure she liked it. She was crazy about it. She practically screamed when she saw the box."

"Oh."

"She promised to make a shirt for each of us, the first thing. Like, you know, that kind of Mexican shirt, with stripes?" Ed hesitated. "I never had anything like that. Do you think it would look dumb?"

"Sure," Rosalie said automatically. "I mean, no! It would look good." She couldn't imagine Ed in a Mexican shirt. That was the kind of thing Tony would look terrific in, with his broad shoulders and his beard. Ed usually wore more stuffy clothes—T-shirts with collars, real pants instead of jeans. Rosalie had often wished he'd dress more interestingly. Now she realized it didn't matter. Whatever he wore, Ed would still just look like a kid.

"You baby-sitting any other day this week?" he asked as they reached the Carlsons' block.

"I don't know. I hope not."

"Well, let me know if you are, so I can walk with you. I almost missed you today."

"O.K."

Ed touched her arm. "There's going to be a square dance at the Ecology Store Saturday. Want to come?"

He worked at the store two afternoons a week, answering phones and stuffing envelopes. Only a couple of volunteers were teen-agers; most of the people were adults. There was a party in the store every month or so. Rosalie enjoyed going to them with Ed, except when there was square dancing. She hated to dance with Ed. She felt terribly conspicuous, towering over him. And it wasn't any better when they changed partners—most of the men in the organization were middle-aged and dumpy.

"Well, do you?" Ed persisted.

"I don't know." Rosalie was hoping there might be another party at the trailer. A party that they'd *ask* her to. "The thing is, I might have to go back to the trailer that night."

"How come?"

"I don't know. I just might. See, I'm going there for dinner Thursday—"

"You planning to move *in* with them or something?"

He was hurt, just as she'd predicted. "Of course not. It's just, they're really nice, and they don't have that many friends in Vandam yet. And sometimes they need to borrow stuff, that I can get for them." Rosalie knew she wasn't making sense.

"I bet they don't really even care about you. They probably just want to borrow stuff you have. And get in good with the neighbors." Ed spoke with surprising heat. "Why would people their age want to be friends with a kid like you?"

Rosalie flushed. "They *like* me! They said so. I even went over yesterday and helped Jill clean up after the party." This was just what she had hoped to avoid. She knew Ed wouldn't understand.

"That's what I mean," he said, smugly. "See, they're probably giving you the big come-on so you'll help them out with stuff. I bet they feel smart, making friends with a kid in the neighborhood. So Mrs. Cree and your mother will think they're nice people. You know what that is? It's exploitation. They're just exploiting you." He looked proud of this interpretation.

Rosalie was furious. "You don't even know them at all—what makes you so snotty all of a sudden?"

"I'm sorry, Rosie," Ed said right away. "I'm probably just jealous or something." That was just like him. He always told you how he felt.

"Listen, what about it?" Ed asked again. "You want to come to the square dance or not?"

"I don't know," Rosalie said lamely. "Honestly, Ed, I just don't know yet."

He stepped back from her, frowning. "Well, excuse me. Excuse me for even asking." Then he shifted his books and started to walk away.

"Ed—"

"See ya around," he called over his shoulder without stopping.

Rosalie walked slowly up the Carlsons' gravel driveway. The thing about Ed was, he was so sensitive. If he could just relax and be cool, like other kids. Anyway, this time he was wrong. Exploitation! That was what mine owners did to the workers, in her social studies book. How could he say such a thing about Jill and Tony and her?

She walked past the huge magnolia blossoms on the small staked tree in the middle of the Carlsons' yard without even seeing them. She felt troubled and angry. She was not going to let Ed interfere with her life. But it felt awful to fight with him. It seemed as though all she did these days was fight! She was already worried about facing her mother tonight. Now she'd have to worry about Ed, too. It wasn't fair.

The front of the Carlsons' house was as carefully landscaped as a house-paint advertisement. Every bush and shrub was pruned so it fit in with the ones next to it. Rosalie thought about the scraggly mess in her own back yard and the bare, ugly ground around the trailer.

The front door opened and Eric hurtled out.

"Rosalie!"

He ran at her with his arms wide open, bumping full-tilt into her stomach.

Rosalie bent to hug him. His hair shone gold in the sun. He smelled of graham crackers and peanut butter. She felt a rush of love for his small, compact body.

"Hi, hon. How are you?"

Eric wriggled out of her hug. "Come on, Rosalie. Hurry up. 'Supermarket Sweep' is on. It'll be over if you don't come right away."

Mrs. Carlson came to the door, looking heavy and

tired. "Hello, Rosalie. How are you?"

"Fine, thanks. How are *you?*"

Mrs. Carlson looked meaningfully at her over Eric's head. "I'm glad you asked that question," she said aloud. Then she mouthed the word "baby."

"Now?" asked Rosalie, startled.

"Any time."

"Hurry up, Rosalie!" Eric tugged at her.

Mrs. Carlson reached out and pulled him to her in an awkward hug. Eric wriggled a minute, then leaned back against his mother's huge stomach while she smoothed his hair. Framed in the doorway, they looked as still and calm as a photograph of a mother and child. Rosalie was touched.

Mrs. Carlson pushed Eric softly away. "Go and watch your program by yourself a while, honey. I want to talk to Rosalie for a minute."

Rosalie expected Eric to protest, but he responded as quietly as a child in a book about children's behavior. "Come and watch with me soon, Rosalie," he said, and went quietly down the hall to his room.

"I will, I promise," Rosalie said after him.

She followed Mrs. Carlson into the white living room.

"It's the strangest thing," Mrs. Carlson began right off, in the confidential tone of one adult talking to another. She sat down carefully on the white couch. "I've been waiting and waiting for this pregnancy to be over, but now that it's really time for the baby to be here I can hardly bear to think of going away from Eric." She laughed apologetically. "I know that must sound funny to you. People have two children all the time. If it was so awful, why would anyone do it?" She sighed. "It's too late to worry now," she said ruefully. "It's ordered."

Rosalie was pleased that Mrs. Carlson would confide in her like this.

"Sometimes I just lie awake nights worrying," she went on. "I know he needs special loving at a time like this, instead of me jumping on him all the time because I'm tired and upset." She leaned toward Rosalie almost pleadingly. "I do so want him to be happy—"

"If there's some way I can help—"

"Oh, Rosalie! You don't know what a help you already are, just loving Eric the way I know you do, and him loving you so much." She shifted her weight on the couch cushion. "What I wanted to ask you is, whether you can come and take care of Eric while I'm in the hospital? Mrs. Reese around the corner says she'll take him home with her Johnny after nursery school. Now, if you could pick him up there and stay with him till Mr. Carlson gets home from work—" She broke off. "It seems like such a lot of arranging!"

"Sure, I can." Rosalie thought wistfully of her afternoons at home, watching Tony and Jill. But she felt sorry for Mrs. Carlson, who had tears in her eyes as she perched sadly on the couch in her brightly striped maternity dress.

"I'll be glad to," Rosalie said. "Eric and I can have a good time together." She wondered if she should ask about the money now. It seemed unfair to take advantage of Mrs. Carlson at a time like this. Still, she ought to try. It would make things so much better with her mother. And she deserved more money. Mrs. Carlson depended on her.

"That's not all we need to arrange," Mrs. Carlson went on. "I wondered whether you'd consider working more regularly over here this summer, when your school's out? Something like three days a week? It would help me so much to have you here when I'm busy with the baby. You could give Eric the special attention he'll need."

It was a real job offer! "I'd like to," Rosalie said.

Mrs. Carlson looked relieved. "Oh, Rosalie," she said warmly. "That's such a load off my mind! I've been afraid to even ask you, for fear you couldn't do it, or wouldn't want to, or something. You can't imagine the crazy ways I worry these days." She leaned forward. "Now, we have to talk about money. I want to pay you decently—after all, you'll be in charge of two children some of the time. What do you think would be fair?"

This was her chance. Rosalie hesitated. She thought of what her mother would say—"Don't sell yourself cheap"—and took a breath.

"My friend Judy said she's going to make two twenty-five an hour at the Grand Union this summer. I think I should get more than that, because it's more of a responsibility, with kids." She felt tense, but proud of herself for coming out and asking.

"You're right," Mrs. Carlson said right away. "It *is* a responsibility. It's worth a lot to me to have someone here that I can trust. How would two-fifty an hour be?"

"That would be great!" Rosalie felt businesslike and excited, too. Wait till she told her mother!

"All right then," Mrs. Carlson smiled. "And we'll start right now, this afternoon." She pushed herself up from the couch. "I want to pay you for this little talk. It's been such a comfort to me. And then maybe you'll stay and play with Eric a while. He's been so good about leaving us alone."

"Thanks, Mrs. Carlson. I'm really looking forward to the baby." For the first time, it seemed real.

"So am I, let me tell you. It's going to be a lot of work, but awfully nice, too, once it gets *out* of here."

Eric burst into the room. "Guess what, Rosalie! A man pushed his shopping cart into a big pile of dogfood cans, and all the cans fell down on him!"

"You know what?" Rosalie took his hand. "When my school's over, and your school's over, I'm going to come here and spend more time with you. Won't that be good?" She stroked his neck, where the hair curled up. "And by then your new baby will be here."

"Yeah. Maybe a boy baby, maybe a girl," Eric said matter-of-factly. "*Now* will you come watch TV with me?"

Rosalie and Mrs. Carlson smiled at each other over his blond head.

"I'm coming," Rosalie said. "But let's not watch TV, O.K.?"

She felt more responsible for him already. She would take such good care of him that he wouldn't even feel jealous of the baby. She would do the best job she could —not just because of the money, but because she loved Eric so much. Already, she felt more at home in the Carlsons' house. They really needed her!

She helped Eric lay out a farmhouse scene on his bedroom rug. They put pigs in the pasture, cows in the barn, and cowboys in the bunkhouse. The cowboys sang "Home on the Range" in Eric's sweet high voice. They were making a corral for wild ponies when Mrs. Carlson came in to say it was time for Eric's supper.

"Can Rosalie stay and eat with me?" he asked.

"Well. . . ." Mrs. Carlson looked questioningly at Rosalie.

"Oh, hon, I can't," Rosalie said, thinking about Tony and Jill for the first time in hours. "I have to go home. I have to get supper for my mother."

"Your *mother?*" Eric looked incredulous. "Do you have a mother, Rosalie?"

Rosalie laughed. "Sure. Everybody has a mother, silly."

"You know who my mother is—that's your Grandma Miller," Mrs. Carlson said.

Rosalie thought about the whole chain of it: mothers and children and mothers and children, going on and on and on. It was astonishing. It was hard to believe that her own mother was going to be a grandmother in a few months. She wondered if Joanne and Joe Pat were getting excited like Mrs. Carlson.

Mrs. Carlson handed her some folded bills. "I do thank you for everything, Rosalie. You've been such a comfort. I think we shouldn't make another date, right now. I'll just call you the minute something happens." She sighed. "Or if it doesn't happen—then I'll probably call you for sympathy!"

Rosalie hugged Eric, and to her surprise Mrs. Carlson hugged *her*. For a minute they stood quietly by the door, touching and peaceful.

The peaceful feeling lasted while Rosalie walked home in the soft evening light. But near her house she felt the familiar jumpy sense of expectation. What were Jill and Tony doing? What had she missed?

When she got to her yard she looked next door. Ken's van was parked behind the blue VW. She went straight to the kitchen window and looked out at Jill and Tony and Ken in a triangle on the trailer steps.

Rosalie felt a stab of jealousy that wiped out her pleasure in the talk with Mrs. Carlson. She remembered all the bad things that had happened today: the fight with her mother, the fight with Ed, the way she had

forgotten to ask about Judy's play. She was resentful of
the cool way Tony and Jill sat out there laughing with
Ken. They probably had forgotten all about her.

Deliberately, she lifted the plastic trash bag from the
garbage can and carried it out the back door. Very slowly,
with her back to the trailer, she lifted the lid of the outdoor can, stuffed the plastic bag inside, put the lid back
on, and adjusted it till it locked in place. She waited for
one of them to look up, notice her, and call her over.

Nobody called.

Furious with herself, Rosalie went inside. Keeping her
eyes away from the window, she took a package of hot
dogs from the refrigerator, washed some potatoes and
put them to boil, and began to scrape some carrots. She
was suddenly ravenous. She resisted the impulse to eat a
piece of bread, and cut up two bananas and an orange for
dessert instead. She would eat one hot dog, half a potato,
and a dish of fruit for supper. She wondered whether
she could have lost weight already.

She pulled the chairs away from the table and began
to sweep the kitchen floor. She was almost finished when
Rita came home with a bag of groceries in her arms.

"Oh, hon, that looks nice." She set the groceries on
the table.

"Guess what, Mom? Mrs. Carlson wants me to baby-
sit three days a week when school's out. For two-fifty an
hour!"

Rita beamed. "Now that's the kind of news I like to
hear at the end of a hard day. That's wonderful, Rosalie!
Two-fifty an hour, say eight hours a day—oh, that's
gonna be a big help. That's practically sixty dollars a
week!" She laughed wryly. "You'll be making more than
me if you keep it up. What got into Mrs. Carlson all of a
sudden, anyway?"

"She was so nice today, Mom. She said she worries so much about Eric, about how he'll feel when the baby comes."

"I don't know what she has to worry about, a fancy place like that and nothing to do but take care of the two kids—*with* help," Rita said. "I would've been happy for problems like hers when I was raising you and Joe Pat, believe me. Still, give credit where credit's due. She's giving you decent pay." She looked at the stove. "You got the supper all cooking, too? Boy, you make me feel like the Queen of Sheba tonight, with the floor clean, food on the stove. And then the money that's gonna come in regular all summer long. We ought to celebrate, go out to the Dairy Queen or something."

"Mom, I decided to go on a diet."

"Rosalie! That's the best news of all. They say bad news comes in threes; maybe good news does, too. Wait'll I tell Maxine!"

"Do you have to tell her?"

"Why not?"

"I don't know. Just, I wish I could do it in private. Without people watching me, counting up everything I eat."

"Rosalie, you know Maxine wouldn't bother you. She'll be glad, that's all."

Rosalie didn't argue. She served the food and she and her mother ate companionably. It was a wonderful change from this morning. When they were eating dessert, Rosalie heard Ken's bus start down the driveway.

At least they didn't ask him for supper, she thought. And they did ask me. She could hardly wait for Thursday to come.

13

But when Thursday came, Rosalie wished it were farther off. She wondered what they would talk about for a whole evening. She was afraid that she might bump into the table or knock over a glass in the small kitchen. Worst of all, she hadn't turned thin. Looking in the mirror, she could imagine that her stomach was a little bit flatter, but the bathroom scales hovered dishearteningly between her old weight and one pound lower.

At five thirty Thursday evening, Rosalie searched desperately through her closet one more time, wishing that something special would appear among her clothes. The shirt and jeans she had ironed so carefully after school didn't look right at all; the shirt was too short in the waist and the jeans seemed to bulge in front. Finally, she pulled an old black turtleneck from the back of her closet shelf. She could wear it out over the jeans to cover the bulge. The black cotton was gray from many washings, but at least the high neck was sophisticated. Rosalie pulled it over her head, ignoring a small ripping sound as she tugged at the shoulder.

The back door slammed, and there were voices downstairs. Maxine had come to eat supper with Rita. They were going to cut out the pants suit afterward. Rita had made this arrangement after Rosalie, who had worried all week about explaining the invitation, finally brought it up on Wednesday.

"I can't see why you want to hang around over there,"

Rita had grumbled, "instead of spending time with your friends your own age."

"It's not 'hanging around' just to eat one meal with them."

"Why don't you ever have Judy come over anymore? You two on the outs or something?"

"She has rehearsals all the time. She was over a couple of Saturdays ago, when you were working."

"What happened with you and the play? I thought you were going out for makeup crew."

"I still am, probably. I don't know." Rosalie had already decided not to. It would be hard to explain to Judy, as well as to her mother, so she had put it off. But she was determined not to tie up her nights with the play. What if Tony and Jill asked her to do something and she was stuck at school?

Rita had answered sharply. "Well, if you're going to be out of the way Thursday night, I'll get Maxine over here to work on the pants suit in peace."

Rosalie wasn't sure how much Rita understood about the pull of the trailer on her. But Rita's crossness showed that she was suspicious of something. Her suspicions made Rosalie feel guilty, and then angry for her guilt. What business of her mother's was it? It's my life, Rosalie told herself. I can pick the friends I want.

Now she washed her face very carefully and tried brushing her hair several different ways. Nothing looked right. Giving up, she brushed it until her scalp stung.

Downstairs, Rita complained to Maxine without even trying to lower her voice. "Every time I turn around I catch her staring out the window at that trailer. I don't know what's got into her. It bothers me, honest it does. I don't like her getting involved with people their age, neglecting her own friends. I haven't seen Ed around here for weeks."

Rosalie made a face at the mirror, pulled at her shirt, and went downstairs to face them.

Rita looked at her appraisingly.

"Walking out on us, huh?" Maxine spoke through a mouthful of pins. A length of checked double-knit fabric was spread over the table and she was pinning a paper pattern to it.

"Yeah, well, I guess I should go over pretty soon." Rosalie felt more apprehensive of going at all.

"Where did you dig up *that* shirt?" Rita asked. "You aren't planning to go out like that, are you?" She turned to Maxine. "I'm telling you, I just can't figure kids out. They beg you for new things and then when they have someplace to go they put on some old rag."

"She looks O.K. to me," Maxine said comfortably. "Come over here, kid, let me look at your shirt. Looks like you've got a little rip up there."

She took the pins from her mouth and laid them on the table. Then she rummaged in her plastic bag until she found a needle and a spool of thread. Squinting, she threaded the needle and pulled Rosalie down beside her.

"It won't take a second to sew this up."

Rosalie squatted by her chair. The gentle in-and-out tug of the needle was soothing.

Maxine snapped the thread with her teeth and patted Rosalie's shoulder. "That does it. Now you're all set."

Rosalie moved toward the door. "I won't be late, Mom. Good luck with the pattern."

The phone rang. It was Chris Newman—of all times!

"Listen, Rosalie, are you coming to do makeup or not? Judy said you would, but you never came around.

There's a costume rehearsal just called for tonight. They want makeup and everything. I can't do it all myself. So can you come? At eight?"

"Oh, wow, I can't, tonight." Rosalie felt Rita's eyes on her. "See, I'm just going out—"

Rita banged her scissors on the table. "Rosalie—"

"O.K., then." Chris sounded angry. "I only called because I promised Judy. Don't bother yourself. I'll find somebody who *wants* to do it."

"Thanks for calling, anyway," Rosalie said. She hung up to face her mother.

"Who was that?"

Rosalie couldn't think fast enough to lie. "Chris Newman, about makeup. I told her I couldn't do it tonight."

"Boy, sometimes I wonder about you," Rita started in. "Passing up chances to go out and do something useful, have fun with other kids your age. Instead of running over to that trailer the minute those people whistle. I think you oughta have your head examined, that's what I think." She shrugged. "But I might as well talk to a wall. You've got your mind made up to go."

"Mom, how could I *not* go? They're expecting me. They bought the food and everything by now."

Rita snorted. "I wouldn't expect a banquet, if I was you. Those people aren't about to serve you steak."

"She said she'd make fried chicken!"

"I wouldn't count on it. They might've forgotten all about it by now." Rita picked up her scissors abruptly. "Come on, Maxine. Let's get moving."

Maxine said, "O.K., I think if we pull it around this way just a little more, we can get a fuller cut in the legs." She looked at Rosalie. "What time you due over there?"

"Six thirty." Rosalie was thinking about what her mother said. Could Tony and Jill have forgotten? What if she went over and knocked on the door and they were already eating their own meal?

"You better get a move on, then," Rita said.

"Have fun," Maxine said.

"Don't stay late," Rita warned. As Rosalie closed the door, she could hear her going on. "I just can't figure out what's got into her. . . ."

Rosalie walked slowly across the yard. By now there was a clear opening through the bushes. She ducked through and walked to the trailer steps, trying to invent a reason for being there in case they had forgotten.

From the steps, she could hear them talking inside. She forced herself to knock.

"Hi, Rosalie." Judy opened the door. She looked very small with a yellow pinafore apron tied over her jeans. Rosalie couldn't see Tony at all.

"Come on in," Jill said. "We wondered if you forgot or something."

"Oh, no!" Rosalie said. "I've been looking forward to it all week!" She followed Jill inside. Why did she have to say that?

Tony was stretched out on the couch with a magazine over his chest, just like a husband in a television show. He turned toward her and laughed. "I've been looking forward to it, too. After the tuna fish and the beans and the macaroni, I'm ready for fried chicken."

"Tony!" Jill protested. "Sit down, Rosalie. Tony, for goodness sake take your legs off the couch and give Rosalie room to sit down."

"It smells so good." Rosalie felt better to find she was expected. She sat down carefully at the opposite end of the couch from Tony, leaving an empty cushion between them. She was too embarrassed to look straight at him, but she was very aware of his reddish beard above the open collar of his faded denim shirt. She could see the red hairs on his chest. It made her almost breathless to be this close to him. She wondered what to say.

Jill said, "It's so smoky in here," waving a hand.

Tony got up and opened the door. "We'll give Mrs. Cree a sniff of your chicken," he said. "Want a beer, Rosalie?"

Rosalie started to say no and stopped herself. She didn't want him to think she was just a kid.

"Sure, thanks."

Tony took two bottles from the refrigerator. Rosalie hoped he was going to pour them into three glasses, but Tony opened the bottles and brought them over.

From the kitchen, Jill gave him a look. "Maybe Rosalie doesn't want all that much."

"Just because you don't like it." Tony settled back onto the couch. "Don't decide for the rest of us."

Rosalie took a quick swallow to show Jill he was right. She was surprised at the beer's sour, unpleasant taste. She wondered how you ever learned to like it. She studied the bottle in front of her. It was awfully big.

Tony got up to close the door. Then he went to the kitchen and peered over Jill's shoulder as she carried a heavy pot to the sink.

"Look out, it's hot!" Jill lifted the pot cover. A cloud of steam rose from the sink. Through the steam and the smoke Rosalie saw Tony put his arms around Jill's waist and squeeze her. They stood like that for a minute. Then Jill smiled, detached herself, and began to mash potatoes.

Tony came back to the couch.

Rosalie had finally thought of a way to start conversation. "How do you like it at Carpenter Community?"

Tony made a face. "You really want to know? Not all that much. They've got all these petty regulations about which course to take. The place is so overcrowded it takes half an hour to find a parking space. The library's so jammed you can't find the books you need unless you buy them." He picked up a book that was on the coffee table. "Fifteen ninety-five for a lousy *Introduction to Psychology*. This is Jill's. You wouldn't catch me shelling out that much for a book." He took a drink of beer. "I don't think it's all that great at Carpenter. Don't let anyone con you into going there."

Rosalie was disappointed. She had expected him to say something good about it. After all, if she went to college at all, Carpenter was the most likely place.

Jill held up the potato masher. "But, Tony, if you take advantage of what's there, you can get a lot out of it. Some of the professors are terrific—"

Tony pretended to whisper to Rosalie. "She's got a crush on her professor."

"I do not!" Jill said from the kitchen. "I just mean, you can learn a lot over there if you put your mind to it."

"Yeah, we know," Tony said. "Put your mind to it, give a wiggle, that's how you women get *A*s."

"Tony! That's not true and you know it."

Rosalie was uncomfortable. They seemed to be arguing about something she didn't understand. "Can I help you?" she asked Jill.

"Well, sure, if you want to set the table that would be nice. It doesn't seem right, though, you being the guest and all." She looked meaningfully at Tony, but he didn't move.

Rosalie was glad to leave her beer bottle, still three-quarters full. "What shall I do?" she asked Jill.

"The glasses are up on that top shelf, where I can hardly reach them, if you want to get them down. You don't know how lucky you are to be tall!"

Rosalie reached up for the glasses, hoping that Tony was watching, and that her shirt hadn't pulled up.

"Look at that!" Jill said admiringly. But Tony had gone back to his magazine.

Jill put a bowl of salad on the table. Then she lifted the cover of the skillet and stuck a fork into the chicken. "It's ready," she said. "Tony, come on, let's eat."

Tony picked up the beer bottles and brought them to the kitchen.

"Water, for me," Jill said. "Rosalie, would you rather have water? Or milk? We have milk."

"Oh, no, this is fine." Rosalie took the bottle Tony gave her.

"Sit anywhere," Jill said, pulling out a chair at the end of the table. Tony sat at the other end, leaving Rosalie no choice but the place between them. She sat down, pulling her feet back carefully so she wouldn't bump into Tony's. The table was so small! Rosalie felt awkward sitting so close to them. It seemed almost as though they were the parents and she was the child.

Jill passed the food. "Everybody begin. Don't let it get cold."

Between bites of chicken Rosalie sipped at her beer. It wasn't quite as unpleasant along with food. She hoped she wouldn't get hiccups—or get drunk! She wasn't sure how much a person had to drink before that happened. Her bottle was still more than half full.

Here I am, she told herself. Eating supper in the trailer. She wished she felt more comfortable. She seemed to tower over Jill, and being this close made it hard to ignore how much fatter she was. She tried to sit as still as she could so she wouldn't bump Tony or Jill's knees. She worried that she would spill food into her lap or knock a dish off the table. She could feel the outside of her mouth turning greasy from the chicken. There were funny little white things in the salad and it was hard to pick them up with her fork.

Jill was watching her. "I love bean sprouts in salad, don't you? I got these at the health food store."

"Oh, yeah, I do," Rosalie said. So that's what they were. They had a crisp, cucumber taste.

"I'll give you some to take home," Jill said. "We can never eat the whole bag before they spoil."

Tony spoke to her suddenly. "I bet *you* don't spend all your time studying, Rosalie."

She tried to look straight at his eyes, the way they told you to in magazine articles about how to get along with people. But it was hard to face him directly when they were so close. She was afraid he could see the piece of chicken that was stuck in her teeth.

"I don't study that much," she said. "I have to get good grades this semester, though. I'm going to take the academic course next year, in high school. So I can go to college."

"Where will you go?" Jill asked.

"I don't know. Maybe Carpenter."

"Don't say I didn't warn you." Tony finished his beer and got up, bumping Rosalie's knees. He picked up her bottle, checked it and set it back down. Then he got himself a new bottle from the refrigerator and jammed it down hard against the counter edge. The cap came off and beer sloshed over his shirt.

"Damn!" he said, jumping back.

"If you'd just give in and use a bottle opener, like other people," Jill said. "Where'd you learn that trick, anyway—from Buddy?"

Tony ignored the question. He sat down and waved his bottle at Rosalie. "I'll tell you a secret. What you want to do is get into the Human Services program at Carpenter. Then you can sit and listen to Professor Mc-Dermott rant on. All the girls are crazy about *him*."

Jill flushed. "What *would* you take, Rosalie, if you went to college?"

"I'm not sure." Rosalie felt dumb. It seemed as though she was caught in some argument, the way her knees were caught between theirs under the table. She was afraid she would say something wrong.

"You ought to check out Human Services," Jill said. "It's a good program. You get to work, like in day-care centers or hospitals, and take classes at the same time. I'm starting at the Y's day-care center next month. I even get paid for it. Not much, but still." She looked at Tony.

"Wiping a lot of snotty noses," he said.

"I didn't know you could do stuff like that at college," Rosalie said quickly.

"At Carpenter you can. That's one reason we came here, so I could be in the program."

"That's the only reason," Tony said.

"It was not! You said yourself that business administration's as good here as Strassberg. You know you did!" Jill stopped and laughed awkwardly. "I almost forgot dessert." She got up and took a pie plate covered with whipped cream from a shelf in the refrigerator.

"Now you're talking," Tony said.

Rosalie had eaten nothing all day to make up for this meal. Still, she knew she shouldn't have any pie. But she was determined not to mention the diet; it would just remind them how fat she was.

She stood up to help Jill clear the table. When her back was to Tony and Jill was absorbed in cutting the pie, she emptied her beer in the sink. It was a relief to watch it flow away.

"I baby-sit for this little boy, Eric," she said then. "His mother's going to have a baby soon. I'm going to work for her this summer. Eric's four. He's really cute."

"Don't let her kid you." Tony winked at Jill. "She likes a big boy better."

Rosalie blushed. "Oh, you mean Ed."

"Oh, you mean Ed!" Tony mocked her voice. She felt ridiculous.

"Do you have a boy friend?" Jill asked with interest. "You ought to bring him over."

Rosalie didn't answer. The last thing she wanted to do was bring Ed here. He'd seem like such a kid to them. Besides, he'd be sure to notice how the Judsons argued, and point it out to Rosalie. And she didn't need him to point it out. It already made her uncomfortable.

"The pie's delicious," she said. She could feel the pounds growing with every bite.

"Thank you," Jill said.

They ate it in silence.

Rosalie was confused. She had looked forward to being here like this, close to both of them, for so long. Now she wondered how soon she could go home.

"How about coffee, Rosalie?" Jill asked.

"Oh, no thanks."

"Tea?"

"No, really. Nothing." She shifted in her chair. "I guess I ought to go home soon. I have homework to do."

"You sound like Jill," Tony said. "She has a thing about studying."

"It's just that I want to take advantage of school," Jill said. "What's wrong with that?"

Rosalie pushed her chair back. Standing up in front of them, she felt enormous. The meal sat heavily in her stomach.

"Can I help you clean up?" she asked.

"Oh, no, you're the guest." Jill got up and went to the counter, where she shook some bean sprouts into a plastic bag. "Here. Take these home." She smiled at Rosalie. "You come again, Rosalie. It makes it seem like home, having company." She turned to Tony. "Don't you think Rosalie has a real resemblance to my sister?"

Tony leaned back, looking Rosalie up and down. Then he brought his chair down with a thump. "Around the eyes, maybe."

Rosalie felt a little better.

Jill patted Rosalie's arm and then hugged her lightly, the way grown people did. "Come again, now."

Rosalie wondered if Tony would get up and hug her too. But he waved lightly from his chair. "So long, Rosalie."

Rosalie walked home, reflecting on the evening. She had to admit it hadn't really gone the way she had hoped. A lot of the time she had felt tense and awkward, instead of comfortable like you should with friends. She felt almost resentful at Tony and Jill. If they knew how she'd argued about them with Ed, and got her mother upset, and Judy was probably furious when she didn't show up for the play—

She wished the evening had been perfect. The way she had hoped it would be.

She turned back for a last look at the trailer. Tony and Jill stood close together, silhouetted in the light. The sight of them reassured her. But it made her wistful, too. They had probably forgotten she was even there. They just didn't know how important they were to her.

She went inside and put the bag of bean sprouts in the refrigerator. She'd put them in a salad tomorrow.

"How long does it take to eat a meal over there, anyway?" Rita called from the living room.

"I left as soon as I could." Rosalie went in to her mother. "Did you finish the cutting?"

"Yeah. Just now. It wasn't easy, getting it all out of that piece of goods. I probably should've bought more, but I hated to. Those patterns always ask for more than you really need. Thank goodness for Maxine. She's a miracle worker." She put her head back against the brown chair. The pattern was on the table beside her.

Rosalie bent down to look at it. "I bet it's going to be nice."

"Rosalie! Have you been *drinking?*"

Rosalie moved away. "I just had a little taste of beer, just one swallow. I didn't like it, honest. I hated it!"

"I told you before, those people are too old for you," Rita said. "Forcing beer on you. Next thing it's gonna be marijuana, who knows what?"

Rosalie could feel the beer and the cream pie rising in her stomach. "They're not like that, Mom. They're just ordinary people. Like Joe Pat and Joanne." She felt close to tears. "Oh, Mom," she said, as the whole strange evening went through her head. "Oh, Mom, I miss Joe Pat so much!"

Gently, Rita reached out and pulled Rosalie down next to her in the big brown chair. "I know you do," she said, stroking Rosalie's hair away from her face. "I do, too." She shifted to give Rosalie more room. "And what am I gonna do, tell me that, when *you* pack up and leave home?"

Rosalie knew she didn't expect an answer. Wedged close to her mother in the chair, she felt a deep relief as her tears came.

For a long time they sat together wordlessly, uncomfortable and close.

14

Heavy rain was splashing against the window when Rosalie woke from confused dreams in which Tony and Jill were teaching her to ride a wobbly bike. She lay half-awake for a moment, looking at the rain. Then she got slowly out of bed. Against the gray sky, the leaves of the apple tree looked like bright green dabs of paint on a black-and-white photograph.

The lilac had flowered overnight, its tight buds opening into small white flower heads that shook in the rain. They reminded Rosalie of other springs, when a thick curtain of pine branches, silvery with rain drops, had swayed behind the lilacs.

Rosalie stared through her blurry window and thought about last night. She wished she didn't feel so let down. They had been nice to her, treating her like a guest. But that was all she had been—a guest. Tony and Jill were a couple, with their own place and their own way of talking—even their own arguments, which she hadn't understood. For the whole evening, it had been like them and her—not the three of them together. Rosalie wondered if it would ever really be the three of them.

She dressed quickly and went to the mirror. As usual on a wet day, her hair was hopelessly wild. As she brushed it, it seemed to her that the reflected girl holding a hairbrush looked thinner. After all that chicken and cream pie—and beer, too! She would have to make up for it today.

Downstairs, Rita poked impatiently at the toaster with a fork. "This darn thing never pops up right. I'm gonna have to give in and buy a new one one of these days."

Rosalie gave her mother a quick hug.

"Sleep well?"

"I sure did. There's something about a spring rain that makes you sleep so nice."

Rosalie poured herself some orange juice, looked longingly at the muffins and jelly, and shut the refrigerator door.

"Know what Maxine said?" Rita asked, buttering her toast.

"What?"

"When I told her about your diet. She said, 'I could've sworn that girl looked thinner already.'"

"That's nice." Maybe it really was starting to show! She wondered if Jill and Tony would notice soon.

They ate in comfortable silence.

"Those kids next door are gonna get flooded out if it keeps on raining like this," Rita said. She sounded almost motherly. "Those kids" was what she called Joe Pat and Joanne. Rosalie wondered if she had made up her mind to accept the Judsons' presence. That would be a relief— as long as she didn't start bossing them around!

Rita dived into the closet for her umbrella. "I don't know what became of our other one," she said. "Maybe you ought to take this. You'll get soaked walking to school."

"It looks like it's slowing down." Rosalie hated to go anywhere carrying an umbrella. It made her feel bigger and more awkward than ever.

Rita peered out. "It's gonna be some mess at the shop today, everybody after me for a specially tight set. 'Give me an extra good hold, Rita!' she mimicked. "If I knew how to make thin hair hold up in the wet, I'd be a millionaire by now." She raised her umbrella and went out. Her car sputtered ominously and then started up.

Rosalie packed her lunch—an apple, an orange, and a hard-boiled egg. It's not really so bad, she thought. Pretty soon I'll be used to it. She imagined herself in a store, trying on a smaller pair of jeans, looking right at herself in the mirror even if the saleswoman was watching.

There was a knock on the door.

"Hi!" It was Jill, in a yellow slicker, with raindrops dripping off her hat. "I came to see if you'd like to drive to some nursery with me today, to buy plants? Now that the ground's so wet."

Rosalie was surprised. She had felt so dumb last night —she couldn't believe Jill would want to see her again. But here she was, asking Rosalie to do something with her. Rosalie was flattered. "I get home at four, would that be O.K.?"

"Sure. Tony wants to stay at the library. We'll have loads of time before I have to go back for him." She sounded excited, like a child looking forward to a treat.

There was a honk from next door. "O.K., O.K.," Jill said. "Coming!" she yelled toward the car, running down the steps. "See ya, Rosie."

Rosalie was pleased that Jill had used her nickname. She gathered up her scarf and books and put on her raincoat. Jill didn't *have* to ask me to go with her, Rosalie told herself. She *wanted* to!

The rain poured down with new intensity as she left the house. She was thoroughly wet before she had reached the Majeskis', where the wooden girl's watering can dripped a steady stream of real water onto soggy tulips. By the time she had reached School Street she was soaked through. She thought she saw Ed coming toward her a block away, under a black umbrella, so she rushed into the building to avoid him. She couldn't stand stumbling along under a shorter person's umbrella. And she didn't want to face Ed. It would be hard to make up without committing herself to go to the square dance with him. She was determined not to tie up her Saturday until she knew what Jill might be planning. But she wished she could tell Ed about their date for this afternoon. That proved Jill wanted her for a friend. Ed just didn't understand.

It was noisy in the dim hall. People stuffed wet coats into lockers and banged the doors shut. Rosalie draped her soaked raincoat over two hooks and headed for the girls' room, working at the wet knot of her scarf.

The room was crowded and steamy. Girls stood in front of the mirrors combing out their hair and balanced against wash basins as they put on lipstick. Rosalie found a spot in back where she could see over people's heads. Her hair had matted down under the scarf. Taking a brush from her bag, she tried to shape it, watching enviously as the girl in front of her pulled a comb easily through sleek blond hair.

"Rosalie!"

Judy came out of a toilet booth.

Rosalie started. "Oh, hi."

Judy's face was set. "I'm mad at you, Rosalie. No kidding. You could have made an effort to come last night. If you don't want to do makeup, O.K. I just wish you'd said so in the first place. Now Chris is mad at me because you didn't show."

"Oh, Judy, I'm sorry. Honest. It's not that I didn't want to." She tried to look at Judy directly. "Just, I had to go out."

"Out where?" Judy pulled her toward the tiled wall.

"To the trailer, for dinner. Remember? I told you they asked me."

Judy made a face. "Did you really have to? I mean, it was like an emergency last night. Everybody was jammed up in the dressing rooms. Rehearsal started about an hour late. It was so embarrassing, because I'd been putting Chris off, covering up for you, and then when you didn't come—" She grabbed Rosalie's arm. "What's going on with you, anyway? It seems like you don't care about anything except those dumb people in the trailer."

"They're not dumb," Rosalie protested. She opened her bag and put her brush away.

Judy was staring at her angrily.

"I said I'm sorry," Rosalie repeated.

"You ought to be! Pam told me you walked right past her yesterday without saying Hi. She thinks you're getting stuck-up just because you met those people. She says they must be desperate, robbing the cradle for friends."

"Since when do you and Pam go around talking behind my back?"

"Since when do you act so crazy? Since when do you say you'll do something and then not even show up?"

Several girls were watching them. Rosalie hunted for words. "Just leave me alone, O.K.?"

"Yes, I will," Judy said. "Gladly." She walked out the door without looking back.

Rosalie went through the day in a fog, trying to avoid Judy in the halls, looking over her shoulder for Ed, hoping she wouldn't bump into Pam. She felt safe in her back seat in English class, until a messenger came in with a note.

Mrs. Miller read it aloud. "Rosalie Hudnecker, please report to the office."

What now? Rosalie wondered as she walked tensely

through the empty halls. Is Mrs. Johnson after me about my program? She was sure she had kept up with her assignments.

"I'm Rosalie Hudnecker," she told the woman behind the counter.

"Who?"

"Rosalie *Hudnecker*." Why did they always make you say it twice?

"Oh, yes. There's an emergency message for you somewhere." She shuffled through the papers on her desk.

Rosalie panicked. What if something had happened to her mother?

The woman held up a pink phone slip. "I don't know what people think, that they can disrupt school routines for every little thing."

Rosalie read the message: *Rosalie Hudnecker, 8th Grade. Call Mr. John Carlson, 866-2450.*

"Oh!" She knew what it meant immediately. "Can I use your phone?"

"There's a pay phone down the hall," the woman said coldly.

Rummaging for a dime, Rosalie ran down the hall and dialed hurriedly.

"It's me, Mr. Carlson. Rosalie."

"Yes, Rosalie. It's good news. Mrs. Carlson had a baby girl this morning!"

"Oh, that's wonderful! Congratulations!"

"We're very happy. Now, Rosalie, will you be able to pick Eric up at Mrs. Reese's this afternoon?"

Oh, no! Just when she'd made the date with Jill. Why couldn't the baby have waited a day?

"Sure," she said, trying to think. "I'll come over a little bit after school's out." She wondered if he knew what time that was. How could she get in touch with Jill?

What if she couldn't? Abruptly she brought herself back. "How's Mrs. Carlson?"

"Fine. And so's the baby. We've named her Karen."

"Oh, I think that's beautiful!"

"I'll tell her you said so."

Suddenly Rosalie thought about Eric. "How's Eric?"

"Pleased, I think. When I called him at the Reeses' he seemed more excited about blueberry pancakes than the baby. Rosalie, I'll get home as soon as I can this afternoon. Thanks a million."

Rosalie leaned back in the phone booth and stared into the corridor. It was so good about the baby! She couldn't wait to give Eric a special hug. But the date with Jill was so important. It was so nice that Jill had asked her. It would be a chance to really talk. How could she give it up?

The end-of-school bell rang. Rosalie got her damp raincoat and pushed her way to the school door. The rain had stopped, but the sky was dreary.

Rosalie went down the steps thinking of Mrs. Carlson's tearful gratitude last week. "It's such a help to know you'll be there," she had said. Mrs. Carlson counted on her. And Eric needed her. He must be so excited! I ought to get him a present, she thought, delaying her decision. She crossed the street and hurried to the card and gift shop on the next corner. The bell on the door rang behind her, making her jump.

"I'm looking for something for a little boy," she told the woman behind the counter. "Maybe a book."

The woman waved toward a shelf of children's paper-backs. Rosalie scanned the titles. Nothing was right. Discouraged, she looked up and saw a rack of thin picture books. *Cowboy Small* was on the top row.

"This is perfect," she told the store woman. "It's just

what he would like." She chose a package of wrapping paper and a spool of red ribbon. The store woman found a pair of scissors and let Rosalie wrap the package on the counter.

"The baby's name is Karen," Rosalie said, as the store woman held her finger on the bow.

"Isn't that pretty? And aren't you the sweet girl, to buy the little boy a present."

Her approval made Rosalie feel worse as she left the store and, doing just what she had feared she would do, turned toward home.

Jill and I won't be gone long, she reassured herself, walking fast. As soon as we get the flowers I'll go straight to the Reeses'.

But Jill's car wasn't in the driveway. Rosalie's heart sank. If Jill was late that would make everything worse. Rosalie tried to imagine Eric playing contentedly with Johnny Reese.

Among the circulars in the mailbox there was an envelope addressed in Joe Pat's writing. Rosalie hurried inside to open it.

> Dear Mom and Rosie,
>
> How are you? We are both fine. You should see Joanne, she gets bigger every day. I tell her she looks like the Circus Fat Lady. (I'm only kidding. She looks real good.) I am putting in lots of overtime, ten hours last week. Guess what, Joanne got a part-time job keeping books for the restaurant downstairs. She works at home and they pay real good ($3.50 per hr.). So we are putting away money for the baby. If things slow down at the garage we will try to get down and see you. Mom, how is work? Rosie, how is school? Well, that's all for now.
>
> Love, Joe Pat

Rosalie wished sharply that Joe Pat was sitting in the kitchen this minute. She wondered if he would think she was different. She felt years older than just last summer, when he and Joanne drove away and she stood behind in her pink dress, waving, until the car turned a corner and she realized they were gone.

Jill drove in next door, jumped out of the car, and ran into the trailer. Rosalie propped the letter against a glass, where her mother would see it, ran her hands through her hair, and rushed outside. If they didn't stay at the nursery too long, she'd be at the Reeses' by close to five. She wondered what time Mrs. Reese expected her. Mr. Carlson hadn't actually said.

Jill ran down the steps. "Hi, Rosie! All set? I took ten dollars from the housekeeping money so I feel good and rich. Not that I'll spend it all."

"Guess what?" At last she had a friend to share her news. "The people I sit for had their baby! They called me at school."

"That's wonderful!" Jill said enthusiastically. "What was it?"

"A girl. Her name's Karen. Karen Carlson."

"Isn't that cute!" Jill opened the car door. Then she straightened up. "Hey—doesn't that mean you have to take care of their little boy?"

"Not right now," Rosalie said uncomfortably. "He's at a neighbor's. They asked me to pick him up later."

"You sure? We could do this some other day."

"It's O.K.," Rosalie said, climbing awkwardly into the small car. She felt depressed already, and they hadn't even started. How did she get herself into so much trouble? Half the things she said these days were lies.

15

"I've really been looking forward to this!" Jill fastened her seat belt, started the engine, and looking back over her shoulder, aimed the car expertly down the driveway.

Rosalie snapped her seat belt and leaned back, feeling locked in. The trip would only take an hour; she wished she could just relax and enjoy it. Here she was, driving down Cedar Street with a grown-up friend. It was just the sort of thing she had dreamed of for weeks as she watched Jill and Tony drive in and out. But now she couldn't keep her mind off Eric.

Jill accelerated fiercely into third gear, her small body energized.

"I thought we should go to Blauvelt's Nursery," she said over the noise of the engine. "From the ads, it looks cheaper than Green Farms."

Rosalie's heart sank. Blauvelt's was way out by Carpenter Mountain. She adjusted her legs, trying to find room in the small space. She wondered how Tony could sit comfortably.

"Damn it!" Jill downshifted expertly to a stop as a traffic light turned from yellow to red. She sounded as impatient as Joe Pat, who always took red lights as a personal insult.

"My brother might come down to visit soon," she told Jill. For an instant she pictured all of them—Tony and Jill, Joe Pat and Joanne and herself—together in the trailer. It would be like a party. Except, she realized, it would be like the other party; I'd still be the one who didn't belong.

"I bet you miss your brother." Jill spurted ahead at the green light, leaving the car in the next lane behind.

"Oh, I do!" Rosalie blurted out, wishing she could explain everything to Jill right then—about the woods, about old times with Joe Pat, even about how much she wanted to be close to Jill and Tony. She was sure Jill would understand.

Jill glanced quickly into the mirror and switched lanes, cutting expertly in front of another car.

"Did you learn to drive in school?" Rosalie asked, envying Jill's competence. When she learned to drive, she'd have her mother hovering over her. That would spoil everything.

"Yeah. In Driver Ed. But they only had automatics. Dad taught me to shift." She laughed. "You wouldn't believe what a back-seat driver Mom was, though. Always telling me to slow down. I guess that's why I love to go fast, now that she's not here to nag me."

Rosalie could hardly imagine Jill with a nagging mother. She seemed so independent.

Accelerating, Jill passed a large truck. They were almost at the edge of Vandam. Beyond a row of peeling billboards, wide fields stretched off toward the hills.

"There's Carpenter Mountain." Rosalie pointed out her window. "It's a neat place for picnics." She wondered if she would ever go there with Tony and Jill. "The turn-off for the nursery's coming up in a minute, where that sign is."

Jill moved into the right lane, downshifting smoothly into the turn. She pulled up between two parked cars and jumped out. "Look at the flowers!"

The big clock on the nursery roof already said four

thirty. Rosalie looked away quickly and followed Jill to the rows of petunias in wooden flats. Jill crouched down to peer among them. She picked out plastic packs and set them back. Rosalie watched her, wishing she would make up her mind fast.

"They look so good all bunched up," Jill complained. "But every pack has broken stems or a plant missing or something." She reached over into the middle row and worked a pack loose. "Here's a good one."

To speed things up, Rosalie began to search with her. "How about this one?"

Jill examined the pack she held up. "No, see, there's a broken plant on this side."

"Oh, yeah." Rosalie began to search more frantically.

"Here's one," Jill said after a while. "Now, just one more."

Triumphantly, Rosalie pulled out a pack covered with velvety blue flowers.

"That's great!" Jill stood up and brushed off her knees. "Now for some red ones."

As carefully as before, she chose three more packs. Rosalie looked up at the clock; it was ten minutes to five. Maybe she should try to call Mrs. Reese.

"Now, some geraniums!" Jill headed eagerly toward the greenhouse. "A dollar-fifty each!" she exclaimed, reading the sign. "They used to be three for a dollar, back home." She laughed ruefully. "That's getting to be a long time ago, I guess. Practically olden times." She pulled out one pot and then another. "There. I can't wait to set them in. It's going to look so nice."

They carried the pots to an outdoor counter. The nurseryman smiled paternally at Jill.

"That it, ladies?" He began to punch the register. "Three reds, three blues, and two geraniums—" He looked up. "There's a special on today, three geraniums for four dollars."

Jill hesitated. "Oh, I didn't know. I guess I ought to take advantage of it."

She ran back to the shed. Rosalie looked around anxiously for a phone.

"Relax, honey," the man said. "What's your hurry, a beautiful day like this?"

Rosalie blushed, afraid to look at the clock.

"Your girl friend here's in a rush, it seems like," the man said as Jill came back with the third geranium. He pulled a cardboard box from beneath the counter and began to fit the plants into it.

Jill turned apologetically. "Oh, Rosalie, is it getting late for you? Will the little boy be waiting?"

"It's O.K.," Rosalie said quickly, trying not to sound tense.

Jill paid for the flowers and carried them to the car. She wedged the box into the back seat and rolled up the windows.

It was five ten when they drove away.

Rosalie leaned back against the headrest. There was nothing she could do about the time now.

The car was stuffy with the windows shut. The pungent smell of the petunias made her feel almost sick. What if Mrs. Reese had called the Carlsons to say she hadn't arrived?

Jill drove home faster than she had come out. At first, she talked enthusiastically about the plants. Then she fell silent, concentrating on stoplights and turns as they neared Vandam.

"That smell sure makes me homesick," she said after a while. Her voice sounded strained. "I—"

Rosalie glanced over quickly. How could Jill be homesick, when she had her own wonderful home?

"I'll take you right to your baby-sitting," Jill said.

Rosalie remembered Eric's book. "Oh, no! I bought a present for Eric, and it's at home." It would take ten extra minutes to go back for it, but she had to get it. Buying that book was the only good thing she'd done all day.

"That's O.K.," Jill said, turning. "We'll go home for it and then I'll take you right where you're going."

The short drive seemed to last forever. Rosalie rushed into her house for the present and climbed back into the car, clutching the wrapping so tightly that shreds of paper came off in her damp hands.

She directed Jill to the Reeses' house. "Thanks a lot," she said, stepping out over the seat-belt strap. "It's been fun." But it hadn't been, really. She and Jill had hardly talked at all, and Rosalie had spent the whole time worrying. She should never have gone!

"It was nice to have company," Jill said. "Thanks for coming along." She waved and backed down the drive. "Come over and help me plant them tomorrow," she called out the window. "I'll wait for you."

Mrs. Reese came out of the front door. "Where have you been? I was beginning to worry." She looked at her watch. "It's six fifteen! The boys have been at each other for the past hour." She rubbed her hand over her forehead. "They've had enough of each other, and so have I." She sounded tired and edgy.

"I'm sorry," Rosalie said. "I had to stay late at school."

"I wish you'd called—" Mrs. Reese began, as Eric darted past her and threw himself at Rosalie.

"Rosalie, Rosalie, we have a baby! A girl!"

Rosalie bent down to hug him close. "Congratulations, hon. Now you're a big brother."

He wriggled away as she tried to kiss him, grabbing for the package. "What's that?"

"Something for you, but we'll open it at your house." Rosalie was eager to get away.

"I want it now!"

Mrs. Reese said firmly, "It's time for you to go, Eric. Your daddy's going to come home and wonder where in the world you are." She turned to Rosalie. "I can't seem to do a thing with him," she said, as though Eric wasn't there. "It's been a big day for him."

Rosalie felt a rush of sympathy. The poor kid, waiting for her all afternoon and getting cranky and tired. It was all her fault for going off on that pointless trip with Jill.

"Let's go!" Eric pulled at her leg.

"Just a minute," Mrs. Reese said tiredly. "I have to hunt for your things. I don't know where you threw them."

She went inside.

Rosalie squatted beside Eric. "Did you have fun with Johnny?"

"No." He made a face.

"Well, we'll go right home to your house," she said gently. "You'll feel better at home."

Mrs. Reese came out holding Eric's sweater and his fuzzy rabbit. "I hope you can get him to calm down," she sighed. "Things were so out of control here, I was just about to try reaching his father at the hospital. He'd told me you'd be prompt."

"I'm awfully sorry." Rosalie was upset. If only the time with Jill had been more fun! She should never have gone.

"Well, anyway, you're here now." Mrs. Reese managed a weary smile for Eric. "Bye-bye, dear," she said in a forced voice. "Come again soon." She bent to kiss him, but Eric jumped away.

"Let's go, hon." Rosalie took his hand. It was small and damp and it comforted her as they walked away from the Reeses' house and around the corner to Eric's.

When they were inside, Rosalie gave him the package. "It's for you, to celebrate being a big brother."

Eric tore the paper away, glanced at the book, and threw it down on the couch.

"I wanna watch 'Dating Game'!"

"Don't you even want to read your new book?" Rosalie was crushed. After all that! She picked up the book and opened it to the picture of the cowboy's hat and boots and saddle.

"Look at all the good things this cowboy has!"

But Eric pulled away and ran to his room, where he turned on the television set. The commercial blared out loudly. "Ring around the collar, ring around the collar!" Eric sang along. "Rosalie, you have ring around the collar!"

He jumped up and down on his bed.

Rosalie tried not to be angry. She sat down on the bed beside him. "Let's just watch your program quietly," she said, stroking his hair.

But Eric couldn't sit still. He jumped off the bed, dumped some blocks from his shelf onto the floor, and began to pile them up carelessly. "I'm making a tower for the baby!" he shouted. The blocks wobbled. Eric gave them a quick shove, and they clattered to the floor.

"Oh, Eric!" Rosalie felt like scolding him, but she held herself back.

Eric stood in the middle of the floor. "I want my daddy," he whined.

"Let's go start supper for your daddy," Rosalie said. "He'll be home soon. Then he'll tell you all about your new baby sister."

Eric followed her into the kitchen.

Rosalie found some lettuce in the refrigerator. She pulled a chair to the sink and set a salad bowl on the counter next to it. "You can wash the lettuce for salad."

Eric pulled apart chunks of lettuce and threw them down in the sink. Then he turned the water on hard. One by one, he picked up the dripping pieces and dropped them into the salad bowl.

"Better pour off some of that water," Rosalie said. "Here, you can dry off the lettuce with this towel."

Eric laughed hysterically. "The lettuce had a bath! Come on, little lettuce, I have to dry you off!" He dabbed at the bowl. It slipped off the counter into the sink. "Hey, you bad lettuce! Get back in!" Eric shrieked.

Rosalie sighed. "Now you'll have to dry it over." Just when she wanted to be especially kind, she felt herself becoming irritated.

Eric leaned his chair toward the window. Then he lost his balance and slipped to the floor, the salad bowl in his arms.

"Ow!" He kicked angrily at the table leg. "Pick me up!"

Rosalie bent down.

Suddenly, Eric stuck out his foot and kicked her hard.

"Hey, that hurt!" Rosalie said angrily. Before she could stop herself, she pulled him off the floor and shook him hard. Then she reached out and slapped his thin arm.

Eric's small face stared at her in surprise.

Rosalie watched a bright red blotch spread across his arm. The sound of the slap echoed in her head.

"You hit me! Mean Rosalie!" Eric pulled out of her grasp and ran down the hall, slamming the door of his room.

Rosalie was horrified. How could she have hit him,

just when he needed extra sympathy? With Mrs. Carlson counting on her? What would she think if she knew? With her heart pounding, she went down the hall and knocked on Eric's door.

There was silence inside.

"Eric! Can I come in?"

"O.K.," he called in a muffled voice.

Rosalie opened the door. Eric lay facedown on the bed. His shirt was pulled out of his shorts, leaving a thin strip of his back bare.

"I'm sorry," Rosalie said, touching the bare place. "I'm really sorry."

"Yeah."

Rosalie pulled him up against her and hugged him, rocking back and forth. Eric relaxed against her. Then she picked him up and carried him into the living room. "Well just sit quietly and look at your new book." She sat him on her lap, tucking his shirt in. He felt very small.

" 'Cowbody Small lives on a ranch,' " she began. Eric snuggled against her. She turned the pages slowly, pointing out details in each picture. They were reading calmly when a key turned in the front door.

"Daddy!" Eric jumped down. "Look at the book Rosalie gave me!"

Mr. Carlson lifted him in his arms and smiled at Rosalie. "Wasn't that good of you!" he said.

Rosalie was too ashamed to answer.

Mr. Carlson sat down with Eric and began to tell them about the baby. He said she was small and blond and looked exactly like Eric.

Eric leaned back against his father and smiled.

"You've had a long afternoon," Mr. Carlson said. "We'll take you right home."

Rosalie accepted the money he gave her, unable to

bring herself to say she hadn't worked that long.

In the car, Rosalie studied Eric's sweet face as he sat between them on the front seat. She vowed to herself that she would never, ever, hit him again. She wondered if he would always remember that she'd slapped him.

"I'm going to take tomorrow off," Mr. Carlson said as they reached her house. He smiled down at Eric. "We'll do something special, just the two of us."

"Oh, boy!" Eric shouted. Suddenly, he looked more grown up. Rosalie bent to kiss him as she got out, wondering if he would pull back. But Eric clamped his arms around her neck in a awkward hug.

"I love you, Rosalie," he said.

"I love you too," she said, grateful for his quick forgiveness. She watched the car back away, waving until Eric's face was gone.

Rita was at the kitchen table, still in her uniform.

"Where've you been all this time?" she asked.

"Oh, Mom, the Carlsons had their baby! A girl! I've been with Eric." Suddenly, Rosalie felt tired.

"Isn't that nice!" Rita said. "A little girl!" She pushed her chair back. "So that's where you were."

"I bet the Carlsons are thanking their lucky stars they have someone as responsible as you to help out."

"I guess so." Rosalie felt miserably ashamed.

Rita sat back, reminiscing. "I remember the day *you* were born like it was yesterday. When they said 'It's a girl', I was so happy I just burst out crying." She reached up for Rosalie's hand. "And then I said right off, 'Her name's Rosalie, cause she's sweet as a little pink rose.' "

"I wish I turned out nicer!" Rosalie still felt guilty, but Rita's familiar story was very comforting. She hugged her mother awkwardly, as Eric had hugged her. "I love you, Mom," she said.

16

That night Rosalie dreamed about Ed. In her dream he was taller than she was, and he had a beard like Tony's. But he talked in his usual way. They were walking down a street, and Ed put his arm around her. That was all there was to the dream, but when Rosalie woke up the feeling of tenderness hung on.

She was still remembering it when Ed ran up behind her outside of school and tapped her shoulder.

"Hey, Rosie!"

She turned around, startled by his real smile, which looked as warm as it had in the dream. She squelched the impulse to tell him about it.

"About the dance tomorrow," he said, as though they had never had an argument. "Can you come?"

Suddenly Rosalie knew what she wanted. She wanted to forget about the trailer for one night. She wanted to go out with Ed. And see Judy.

"You know what?" she asked, encouraged by his kind look as much as by the dream. "What I'd really like is to go to Judy's rehearsal. That is, if you wouldn't mind missing the dance." She rushed on, wanting to confide in him. "See, I got into this fight with her because I said I'd help with makeup and then I didn't. I want to show her I really do care about the play."

"Well, sure," Ed said immediately. "I heard the play's fantastic. I'd like to see it too. We can always go to some other square dance. I don't care that much what we do—

the thing is, I just want to do something with you." He smiled shyly.

"Oh, thanks! That's really nice of you, Ed. Especially —" She had to apologize. "I'm sorry I acted so dumb the other day," she said. "I've been getting in fights with everybody, it seems like. I don't know why I've been acting so dopey." I do know, she thought to herself. I've been so hung up on the trailer that I've been just awful to everyone. Guiltily, she wondered what Ed would say if he knew she'd slapped Eric. Could he know? He was staring at her in a funny way.

"You're looking good, Rosalie. That's a neat shirt."

Rosalie looked down in surprise. It was her old navy blue T-shirt that he'd seen hundreds of times. It must be the diet! She pulled herself up straight.

The bell rang. They went into the building together. For once, Rosalie didn't try to hang back so that she could walk a step below him.

"See ya tomorrow." Ed turned to his locker.

"See ya," Rosalie said. The day was off to a good start. Now if she could just get up the nerve to apologize to Judy. It would feel wonderful to get it over with and act natural with her friends again. She missed everybody.

But when she walked into the cafeteria and saw Judy and Pam laughing together at the regular table, she almost lost her resolve. She had to force herself to cross the noisy room and walk up to them.

"Hi."

They looked up.

"Hi, Rosalie," Pam said coolly. Judy didn't speak.

"Look, I just want to say I'm sorry," Rosalie said quickly. She pulled out the bench across from them and sat down so they couldn't turn away. "I was awful about the play, I know. And I've been feeling so bad about yelling at you in the girls' room yesterday, Jude."

"Chris was pretty mad about the makeup," Pam said.

"So was I," said Judy. "You put me on the spot with her. And then, the way you talked yesterday—"

Rosalie forced herself to look straight at her. "I know it. I don't know what got into me. I was feeling so guilty, but I was too ashamed to say so, I guess." She took her orange from her paper bag. "You wouldn't believe how low I felt. I've been hiding out for days, so I wouldn't have to face you, and then when you came out of the toilet I was trapped. Cornered like a crook."

Judy almost smiled. The tension seemed to relax.

"I've missed you guys, you know," Rosalie said.

"Yeah, well, we missed you, too," Judy said back. "Like, I've been dying to show you my costume, but I wasn't going to until you apologized."

"I apologize." Rosalie put her hand on her heart the way she and Judy used to when they made promises in first grade. "I vow not to act like such a dope anymore."

They laughed.

"I'm coming to see your rehearsal tomorrow night," Rosalie said, very glad it was all set. "With Ed."

"Come backstage after, O.K.?" Judy responded at once. "I'll fill you in on all the gossip."

"Judy and Billy Kirchener are a hot item," Pam put in.

"Really, Jude?" Rosalie laughed. She still couldn't think of Billy Kirchener without remembering how he looked back in kindergarten.

"Well, he's a pretty good actor," Judy said complacently. "And he doesn't act so bad offstage, either."

Pam had been watching Rosalie peel her orange. "Rosalie! You're on a diet!"

Judy looked her over. "You know, you're looking terrific. Did you lose weight already?"

"About three pounds, I think." Rosalie enjoyed their stares. She sat up straighter. "It's really boring, honestly. Sometimes I think I never want to see another orange."

"The way you look, it's worth it." Judy set down her milk carton. "So, Rosie—what's been happening? You still hanging around with those people in back?"

"I've been baby-sitting, too," Rosalie said defensively. "Oh, hey, the Carlsons had a girl yesterday!"

"Nice," Pam said. "A boy and a girl, that's neat. Hey, Rosalie, was that her I saw you with in a blue VW yesterday?"

Rosalie was pleased. "Yeah, I went out to Blauvelt's with her." She wasn't going to tell them the trouble *that* had got her into. "She's a fantastic driver," she said, to impress them. Everybody in junior high wished they could drive.

"They still arguing about mopping the floors?" Judy asked.

"They don't argue that much." Rosalie felt deflated. "Half the time they're hugging or something."

"You keeping score?" Pam giggled.

Rosalie flushed.

"I'm glad I'm not them," Judy said. "Stuck in that stuffy little trailer all summer with all the trees cut down."

"You'd really be on top of each other in a trailer," Pam said. "All cooped up."

"They're not cooped up!" Rosalie protested. "It's romantic back there!" The minute she'd said it she knew they'd laugh.

"Romantic!" Judy snorted. "Honestly, Rosie. Do you call a view of Mrs. Cree's underwear on the line romantic?"

Pam and Judy laughed. Despite herself, Rosalie laughed with them. It was just so nice to be silly with her friends again.

But for the rest of the day she felt bad when she thought about what they'd said. She remembered how Jill had talked about being homesick. Could she feel cooped up back there? The idea made Rosalie uncomfortable.

After school she hurried home to help Jill with the flowers. At least, they'd make the trailer look more homey. The driveway was empty. Rosalie took her books inside and read a chapter of social studies while she ate another orange. Then she went out to the garage for the shovel, and rummaged through an old basket of tools until she found a trowel.

She carried the tools across the yard and through the hedge, where fat bees were already buzzing around the lilacs. She laid them on the ground by the box of flowers and sat down on the steps to wait for Jill.

But Mrs. Cree pushed open her back door and started down the steps with a basket of laundry. Rosalie felt exposed on the steps. She got up and pushed against the trailer door. It was unlocked. Jill won't mind if I wait inside, she thought, stepping inside.

In the sunlight, the room looked as sharply real as a stage set before the actors have come. Rosalie looked around her at the little lampshades, the bright cushions and spread, the poster and the bookshelves and the plant in the corner. It was all so familiar that Rosalie could almost imagine she lived here.

Impulsively, she went to the kitchen and filled the small blue teakettle. She lit the little stove and put a tea bag into a yellow cup. When the water had boiled she poured it over the tea and carried the cup to the couch.

She settled back against a pillow, waiting for it to cool. Although she could see her own back steps by bending forward to look out of the window, the room seemed to be part of another world. A romantic world. She relaxed dreamily.

"What're *you* doing here?"

Mrs. Cree stood in the doorway, a bag of clothespins tied to her apron.

Rosalie sat up. "I was just waiting for Jill—for Mrs. Judson."

Mrs. Cree went straight to the sink and yanked at the water faucets.

"I told them before they moved in, always check those faucets. One little drip can run your water bill sky-high."

Rosalie couldn't think of an answer.

Mrs. Cree didn't expect one. "They're nice enough folks," she said. "If it wasn't for that car of theirs tooting up and down the driveway all hours. Better them than some flighty single girl bringing the Lord knows who all back here. The only trouble with two people, it makes twice the expense: lights, gas, water. Twice as many toilet flushes. It all adds up."

She raised a corner of the tablecloth and peered underneath. "A nice formica table, seems a pity to cover it up. Protects it some, I guess. Look at the edge of that counter —all marked up already."

She wet a dishcloth and rubbed vigorously at the place where Tony had opened his beer bottle, shaking her head. "Cut right through." She dried her hands on a dish towel and peered at Rosalie. "They give you a key to the place? I told them to hang on to their keys."

"Oh, no. It was just—the door was open, and I was waiting for Jill."

"You better tell her to keep that door locked. No telling

who might walk in." She went to the door, looking down. "Floor could use a good scrubbing." Then she went out.

Rosalie couldn't help laughing to herself. Twice the toilet flushes! Of all the dumb things. She'd have to tell Judy, she thought, and then changed her mind. It would just convince Judy that she was right about the trailer.

"Rosie!" Jill burst in with a bag of groceries.

"Oh, I hope you don't mind—I just came inside to wait for you."

"I'm real glad you did." Jill put her bag down. "You just gave me a fright, that's all. I thought you were Mrs. Cree! She's always hanging around."

"You just missed her," Rosalie said. "She was here."

"What did she want?"

"I don't know. It just seemed like she was being nosy." The word embarrassed Rosalie. "I hope you won't mind," she said quickly. "I made myself a cup of tea. I guess I just felt at home."

"I'm glad!" Jill said. Rosalie could tell she meant it.

"I brought over a shovel and trowel, to do the plants."

"Oh, that's nice. But you know what? I'd rather if we could just sit and talk for a while." She laughed shyly. "Like back home, when my mother has friends for tea." She reached into the grocery bag and pulled out a package of cookies, unwrapped it and put some cookies on a plate.

"Have a fig newton? They're my favorite. I just saw these in the grocery store and I said to myself, Jill Judson, if you want fig newtons all you have to do is buy yourself some. You don't have to beg your momma; you're a grown-up married lady now."

Rosalie knew exactly how she must feel. Buying any-thing you wanted in a store was a real sign of being grown. She wondered if Joe Pat bought himself lots of Clark Bars, now that he was far away from Rita and

Maxine and their warnings about what chocolate does to complexions. Joe Pat loved Clark Bars.

"I shouldn't have any, thanks." Rosalie looked at the cookies longingly. "See, I'm on this diet. You're so lucky, not to have to worry about what you eat."

"I don't see why you're worried," Jill said right away. "Haven't you lost weight since we moved here? It seems like you're thinner than when I first saw you."

"A little." Rosalie felt good. Everyone seemed to be noticing today.

"I admire you," Jill said. "It must be so hard to stick to a diet. I don't think I would have the willpower." She bit into a cookie. "Excuse me if I sit here and eat in front of you."

"That's O.K.," Rosalie said. The rich fig smell was tantalizing. She took a swallow of tea.

"This is nice." Jill settled back into her chair. "A chance to talk, that's something I miss. With another girl. I don't ever seem to have time at school. I'm always running from one class to another, or stuck in the library with my head in a book." She laughed uneasily. "Maybe there's something wrong with me. Tony seems to pick up people wherever he is."

"Well, with all the studying you have. . . ." Rosalie was surprised to feel sorry for Jill. "What about Lisa?"

"Oh, Lisa works all day and takes night classes, so she's busy. It just takes time to make friends, I guess, and Tony has more of that. He doesn't worry that much about school. I mean, he goes to classes. But he doesn't like to study. That's why he has to stay at the library this week—he's trying to catch up. The way I feel is, I better study hard now. It might be the last chance I get."

"Do you like Carpenter?" Rosalie realized she only knew Tony's opinion.

"I love it! I guess Tony thinks I'm crazy. He wanted me to take a secretarial course so I could earn money right away. But I don't want to get stuck in an office. I want to do some good for somebody." She smiled. "Back in high school, that's how my aptitude tests always came out: Good with People."

"I know how you feel," Rosalie said. It was amazing how alike she and Jill were! "At school they wanted me to go out for the beautician's course."

"Like your mom."

"Yeah." Rosalie leaned forward. "See, Mom's really good at it. Her best friend works in the same shop. All the customers like her. I'm proud of Mom. She raised me and Joe Pat by herself, working at Loretta's. She's really something! I just hope she knows how much I admire her, even if I don't want to be a beautician."

"She probably does," Jill said. "But I bet she'd be glad if you came right out and said it."

"Well, yeah—I guess I should." Rosalie wondered why such a reasonable suggestion should seem surprising. "I just never thought about, you know, saying it, just like that."

"Most people don't," Jill said. "But a thing I've been learning at school is, it's good to say things you feel. I bet you'd like the Human Services course," she went on. "Somebody like you, who's good with kids. They teach you all kinds of stuff about working with people."

"I bet you're good at it," Rosalie said. "Just the way you're talking to me like this. At school, they never really talk to you about what you could do. I have this guidance counselor, but she sort of scares me." Suddenly Rosalie wondered if this was what she had been wishing for all along: somebody to talk to. Somebody older and friendly like Jill.

"Well, I hope I'll be good," Jill said.

Rosalie decided to tell her about Eric. "You know what I did yesterday after you took me to get Eric? I felt sorry for him. I know he was feeling funny about the new baby, and he kept acting silly and jumping around and getting wild. I wanted to be nice to him—and instead, I slapped him!"

Jill reached out and put her hand on Rosalie's. "Oh, I bet you felt awful!"

"I did." Rosalie could see that red splotch spreading across Eric's arm. "But afterward, he acted so sweet. I just hope he won't always remember that I slapped him the day his sister was born."

"I bet he'll remember that you brought him a present," Jill said. "And that you really love him. Everybody gets mad sometimes," she went on. "I know I do. And then I feel so bad afterward. Like when I fight with Tony. And then later I wonder, how can I get so mad at somebody I love?"

What she said about Eric was comforting, but Rosalie wasn't sure she wanted to hear about Jill and Tony fighting. "Mom and I fight all the time," she interrupted. "Like about my hair. She's always after me to get it cut. I think I'd sort of like to, but when Mom starts nagging, I don't know, it just makes me so mad. I don't want to get my hair cut because of her. If I do it, I want to do it for myself."

"I bet you'd look cute with short hair," Jill said. "Yours is so thick, it would probably curl up real nice." She reached over and pulled a bunch of Rosalie's hair to the top of her head. "Oh, I think it would be pretty."

"Maybe I'll do it," Rosalie said, suddenly eager to try. Now that she was getting thinner, it would be fun to look different. If she did it this summer, she'd feel like somebody new when she went to high school. Not like her old shy, awkward self that she didn't want to be anymore. But a person who could talk to people and take care of kids and do well in school. And like how she looked.

"My mom and I used to fight a lot, too," Jill said. "But Mom's really nice, like yours is. In a way," she said, looking around, "it was easier to make up with her than it is with Tony. It's so cooped up in here, it seems like we're on top of each other all the time."

Rosalie thought of what Pam had said.

"I just get upset too easily," Jill went on. It seemed as though she really needed to talk about it. "Like yesterday, when I went back for Tony at the library. He was sitting out on the steps with some girl, not even studying or anything. So I honked and he didn't get up and I honked again, and then this girl yelled 'Take it easy,' and I was so insulted—she didn't even know I was Tony's wife, or care, anyway. When we got home I was so mad I didn't even want to speak to Tony and he turned the TV on so loud he couldn't have heard me if I did. This place is so *teeny!*"

Rosalie didn't know what to say. It was so different from the way she liked to think of them.

Jill smiled wanly. "Oh, Rosie, I'm sorry. I didn't mean to load you down with all that. It just sort of popped out. I guess I've been needing someone to talk to."

Rosalie thought frantically of the scenes she'd watched from her window: the two of them laughing on the steps, throwing a Frisbee around, kissing in the lighted window. Of how magical it all had seemed.

"Ever since you moved in," she blurted out, "when I look at you and the trailer and the way you live, it seems so romantic!"

"Oh, it is," Jill said seriously. "But it's not how I

thought it would be, when I was your age. All that stuff about 'happy ever after.' "

"Happy ever after" was just what Rosalie had wished for. What she had yearned to be part of. She felt as though Jill was spoiling it, by talking like this.

"It's not magic, or anything," Jill went on. "You don't all of a sudden stop wanting to learn things, or make friends, and all that. Everything isn't perfect, just because you're married. You still keep wanting things to change."

"Yeah," Rosalie said, thinking of how she had wished nothing would change. If only they hadn't cut down the woods, she thought. If only—

Jill said, "But it is romantic." She smiled. "You look so sad, Rosalie. Don't let me spoil your dreams."

Rosalie didn't know how to answer. This wasn't anything like her dreams. Everything has to change, she told herself. Even dreams.

Suddenly the trailer seemed very small and stuffy. She felt cooped up. She stood up. "I should go. Mom's going to be home soon."

"Come again soon," Jill said. "It made me feel good to talk to you."

"I will," Rosalie said. It *had* been nice to talk to Jill. She was really a friend. But as she walked home, Rosalie felt depressed. It made her sad to realize how mixed-up her dreams had been.

She was too preoccupied to carry on a conversation with her mother at supper time.

"What's the matter, aren't you going to eat anything?" Rita said, looking at her plate. She laughed. "I never thought I'd see the day when I sat here and told you to eat up."

"I just don't feel that hungry."

"You need to keep up your strength," Rita persisted. "I saw an article in the *Enquirer* today about these young girls who go on diets, stop eating, practically starve themselves to death—"

"Mom!" Rosalie said. "I'm not starving!"

Rita warmed to the subject. "This article told about one girl, wouldn't eat a thing, shrank down to eighty, eighty-one pounds, they had to take her to the hospital—"

"Don't worry, Mom," Rosalie said. "I'm O.K. I can take care of myself."

She hoped it was true.

17

Rita was up early the next day, getting ready for her long Saturday at the shop.

Her alarm clock woke Rosalie. She lay in bed listening to the familiar sounds of water running and drawers slamming. Rita's Saturdays had been like this ever since Rosalie and Joe Pat were small. In those days, her mother used to leave them each a quarter to spend on something special while she was gone. And when she came home, no matter how tired she was, she'd load them in the car and take them to a drive-in movie or to the Dairy Queen for ice cream.

Rosalie felt a rush of sympathy for her mother. She jumped out of bed and dressed quickly, threw some water on her face and ran downstairs to make breakfast. When Rita came into the kitchen in her uniform, the table was set and Rosalie was scrambling eggs.

"Doesn't that look nice," Rita said. "A good start for what's gonna be a long hard day. I'm down for three permanents that I know of, besides the usual Saturday rush."

She looked tired, almost frail. Rosalie set the plate of eggs in front of her and bent down for a quick kiss. "Enjoy it, Mom. You work so hard, you deserve a nice breakfast."

Rita looked up with a quick smile. "Well, thanks, hon. That's a nice thing to say." She took a bite. "A breakfast like this'll last me all through the day. I was gonna work right through lunch time, anyway. I told Maxine, I wanna leave on the dot, get to the fabric store before it closes. September's gonna come before we know it, and Joe Pat's baby won't have any fancy thing to wear if I don't get started."

Rosalie laughed. "You're going to spoil that baby!"

"It won't be near enough for me to spoil," Rita said. "But it's gonna be something, when they bring their little baby down here to visit." She swallowed some coffee. "When's Mrs. Carlson coming home with hers?"

"Monday. I can't wait to see her. I hope she'll like me."

"She'll love you, just the way Eric does."

Rosalie tried to repress the memory of Eric's white face staring at her when she slapped him. He does love me, she told herself. And I'll show him how much I love him.

"The Carlsons' baby's gonna be good practice for you," Rita said. "By the time Joe Pat's baby comes you'll know all about it. You'll be a smart auntie."

"I hope so." Being an aunt seemed so grown-up! Rosalie could hardly believe it would happen.

Rita went to the sink to rinse her plate. "Those kids better set their flowers in before they die," she said, looking out. "What're you going to do all day, hon?"

"Clean house," Rosalie said. "Mop, vacuum, the works. You won't know it when you come home."

"Well, that's nice, hon. Thanks."

"I'm going out tonight, with Ed. To Judy's rehearsal."

Rita smiled. "I'm glad to hear it." She looked at Rosalie almost shyly. "I didn't like to say anything. But it's been worrying me, the way you've been hanging around home. Do you good to get out with the other kids."

"Yeah."

Rita picked up her keys and went to the door. "Don't work too hard."

"You either." But Rosalie knew her mother would be rushing from one customer to another all day long.

She cleared the table and ran water into the sink. Washing the plates, she stared out the window. In the harsh morning sun, the trailer looked as bleak and out of place as when it had first appeared. She could hardly remember how the woods had looked, before. And how excited she had felt when Tony and Jill first came.

The door opened and Tony and Jill came down the steps. Rosalie looked anxiously for a sign of strain between them, but they looked just the same. Rosalie wondered what Jill was thinking. It was hard to believe she had sounded so sad yesterday. Now she smiled at Tony and got into the car. They drove off.

Rosalie tried to push them out of her mind. She turned away from the window, dried her hands, and got out furniture polish and dust cloths. Then she dragged the vacuum cleaner into the living room. Enveloped in its sound, she pushed the hose back and forth across the rug. Then she dusted the lamps and polished the furniture. She looked around the room. Morning sunlight fell onto the painted sunset of *A Woodland Lake*. Rosalie stood in front of the painting, a dust cloth in her hand, caught up in its old magic. Then she pulled down the shades so the room would stay cool. The smell of furniture polish was pleasant. The room wasn't elegant like the Carlsons', or cute like the trailer. But it looked clean and peaceful in the shadowy light.

Upstairs, she scrubbed the bathroom and then, taking off her shoes, she stood on the scales. She had lost four pounds! She cleaned her mother's room and the hallway and started in on her own closet, trying on clothes and pushing the things that seemed loose to the side. She thought happily of buying some new things this summer, when she had regular money from the Carlsons.

She made her bed, smoothing the bedspread carefully over her pillow. On her twelfth birthday her mother, followed by Joe Pat and Maxine, had led her in here with her eyes closed and watched expectantly as she opened them to see the new pink spread and the matching curtains. That seemed like ages ago.

When the upstairs was clean, Rosalie took a shower, put on clean clothes, and brushed her hair. She was startled by the girl who looked back at her from the mirror. I look different, she thought. Older, maybe. She held her hair back and studied the effect. She felt almost ready for a haircut.

Pleasantly tired, she lay down on her bed with her arms beneath her head. Maybe there would be a party somewhere tonight, after the rehearsal. It would be fun to see Judy with Billy Kirchener, and to kid around with her friends. It seemed as though she'd been away from everyone for weeks while she was so caught up with the trailer. As though she had thought about nothing else. I have to think about myself for a change, she thought drowsily, and closed her eyes.

She woke up confused from daytime sleepiness. Automatically, she looked out the window. The VW was in the driveway, and the trailer door stood open. The flowers looked almost dead in their box. I should go over and get Jill to plant them, Rosalie thought. It would be so sad if they died before she got them in. She put on her sneakers and walked across the yard. I'll tell her I decided to get a haircut, she thought. Saying it out loud would make her do it.

She climbed the steps and hesitated at the open door. "Jill?"

There was no answer.

Rosalie stepped inside. "Jill, it's me."

For an instant she wondered if something could be wrong. Then she saw an empty laundry basket by the bedroom door. Jill must be in there, sorting the laundry.

She called toward the door. "Hey, Jill, are you in there? I came over to help you set your flowers in."

The door opened. But it was Tony who came out!

He was wearing a pair of cutoffs and nothing else. His hair was rumpled. He looked as though he had been napping.

Rosalie backed away. "Oh, I didn't know—I came over to see Jill—"

"Hi, Rosalie." Tony brushed at his hair and his beard with his hands, and smiled sleepily at her. "Jill's at the library this afternoon. You caught me—I was sneaking in a little nap before I go to pick her up."

"I didn't mean to bother you," Rosalie said, trying to back toward the door without staring at him. But she couldn't stop herself. Reddish-brown hair curled thickly across his chest, ending in a V at his navel. His shorts began lower than that, beneath a strip of white skin. Rosalie had the curious sense that she was seeing him naked. She didn't know how to leave.

"No bother," Tony said, coming toward her.

Rosalie looked down at his bare feet. They were soft and pink. The reddish hair stopped at his ankles. She caught her breath.

"I was going to help Jill with the flowers," she said.

"I think those flowers have had it," Tony said. "They looked pretty far gone this morning. But Jill didn't want to give up on them. I threw some water at them before I dozed off. Jill said she'd put them in tonight when it's cool." He pointed to the couch. "Come on," he said, as comfortably as though he were fully dressed. "Sit down and have a beer or something."

"Oh, no— I better get home." Rosalie stood transfixed.

Tony rummaged in the refrigerator. "How about a Coke, then?" he asked, as though what they would have to drink was the question. The thought of drinking anything at all, alone with this half-dressed man, made her terribly uneasy.

"I should go," she stammered, wondering why she didn't. "I wouldn't have come, only Jill said to come any time—"

"Well, sure," Tony said pleasantly. "Any time. And here you are, so why not just sit down and relax for five minutes?" He looked at his bare wrist. "Know what time it is? I promised to get Jill at five."

"Oh, it can't be that late—" Immediately, Rosalie was sorry she'd said it.

"Well, then," Tony said expansively. "Come on. Sit down."

Unable to do anything else, Rosalie sat.

Tony pulled the tab from a can of beer and set it on the counter. There were two empties there already. "Aren't you going to drink anything?" he demanded.

Rosalie couldn't think of a reason not to. "If you have a Coke—" She hated the thought of the calories, but it would give her something to do.

Tony brought her one.

Rosalie stared at his bare thighs. She wondered where he would sit.

He slumped easily into the chair across from her.

Rosalie noticed that the room was a mess. The dishes weren't done, and the floor was still dirty. It was hot. With no trees outside and the sun pouring in, the air in the trailer was thick and stuffy. She understood what Jill meant about being cooped up. She felt almost dizzy.

And yet, sitting this close to Tony, she felt a lurch of excitement. She swallowed some Coke, almost choking on the sweet liquid. She wondered what you were supposed to say to your friend's husband when you were alone with him like this.

"I think Jill's so nice," she said.

Tony crossed his leg, putting a bare foot over his thigh. He seemed very relaxed. "Oh, she thinks you're nice, too," he said easily. He looked straight at her. "We both do."

Rosalie shifted under his gaze. She couldn't help wondering how she looked. Could he see that she'd lost weight?

"She's so easy to talk to," she hurried on, feeling that she was babbling. "More than most people." She almost said "most older people."

"Yeah," Tony said. "Jill's great."

There was a silence. Rosalie watched a column of dust motes flickering in the stream of sunshine that fell between them.

"She gets hung up about things, though," Tony said confidentially. "Like, she's got this crush on her professor, and she feels guilty about it so she starts jumping on me, picking on every little thing I do. She acts like I'm fooling around if I even say hello to another woman."

Rosalie knew she didn't want to hear any more. She thought of what Jill had said yesterday, that "happy ever after" wasn't easy. She had a sudden feeling of sympathy for the two of them, working out their difficulties in this little place.

But that was their problem. It didn't have to be hers. She remembered her old dream of the three of them, their arms linked together, laughing along a street. In that dream she had seemed almost like part of them. She had yearned so much to belong. Now she just wanted to get away.

She stood up. "Thanks for the drink," she said, in what she hoped was a grown-up tone.

Tony stood up, too, only a couple of steps away from her. She was immediately conscious of his height, his broad shoulders, his reddish beard. His whole bare body.

"Don't run off," he said, smiling down at her.

Rosalie couldn't decide whether the smile was friendly or brotherly or something else.

He reached out and put a hand on her shoulder. "Don't go," he said again.

"I have to," Rosalie said. "I have to get supper for my mother." She couldn't take her eyes off his chest.

Tony put his other hand on her other shoulder. Rosalie froze. She wondered if he was going to kiss her. She wondered if she wanted him to.

Tony leaned toward her. "You're a good kid, Rosie," he said gently. "I'll tell Jill you came by."

"O.K.," Rosalie said, shaken but relieved, like a heroine who has come safely through a perilous journey. Beyond Tony's shoulder she noticed a chunk of wood-grained plastic peeling from the living-room wall.

"See ya," she said, and backed out the door.

She ran breathlessly down the steps and across the yard. When she reached her own door she leaned against it and laughed in relief.

It could make a good story for Judy. Sitting in the trailer like that, talking with a practically naked man. Tossing her hair back like an actress, she opened the door and went in.

Ed sat at the kitchen table.

Rosalie stared at him.

"Hi," he said in his ordinary voice. "How ya doin?"

"O.K.," Rosalie said, catching her breath.

"Your door was open so I came on in. I tried to call you from the Ecology Store before, but no one answered. I was working there all afternoon, and it seemed dumb to go home. I thought I could eat with you and we'd go to the play from here."

"Sure." Rosalie pulled at her shirt.

"Where were you, anyway?"

"Just—I went over to the trailer to see Jill, but she wasn't there." She wondered if she sounded funny.

Ed didn't seem to notice. "You still go over there a lot?"

"Oh, no," Rosalie said quickly. "Just now and then. I don't like to bother them."

She heard the car driving out next door, but she kept her eyes away from the window. "What time is it, anyway? Is it almost five?"

"Ten of."

"I didn't realize it was that late. I was taking a nap, before I went over there."

"You still look sort of sleepy," Ed said. He seemed to be staring at her.

"Do I?" Rosalie felt as though she'd been asleep for a long time. Asleep and dreaming. But now she felt awake. Ed kept on staring at her. She wondered if she looked any different. She wondered what he was thinking.

"What's for supper?"

Rosalie opened the refrigerator door and looked in. "Mostly cold stuff." She pulled out cheese and lunch meat, hard-boiled eggs and mustard. "How about if we just have sandwiches?"

"Sure, fine," Ed said. "I'll set the table if you want."

"O.K." Rosalie waved toward the cabinets. "You know where stuff is." She began to set the food on plates, feeling calmer as she worked. It felt good to be with Ed in the quiet kitchen.

"It's a long time since I was over," Ed said. "The last time was right after they cut down the pine trees. Remember?"

"I remember." It seemed like years ago.

"What's it like back there in the trailer?" Ed looked out the window. "It sure is bare."

"Yeah. I really miss the trees," Rosalie said.

"I would, too. You don't have much privacy anymore."

"Neither do they," Rosalie said.

"That's for sure. You can practically see right in there from here."

"And Mrs. Cree's always hanging around," Rosalie said. "The other day she walked right in, while I was over waiting for Jill." She was sorry as soon as she said it. He'd think she was always hanging around too!

"I guess you're really getting to be friends with them," Ed said carefully, as though he wanted to know but was afraid she'd get mad if he pressed.

"Oh, I don't know," Rosalie said. "They're nice. I really like talking to Jill. But—" she paused. "They're so old."

Ed reached up for the glasses on the cabinet shelf. Rosalie watched him thoughtfully. He looked very much at home. It was nice to be with him again.

"I'm glad you came over," she said.

"Thanks, Rosie." He set the glasses down on the table, one by one. Then, with no warning at all, he walked over to the counter where she was spreading out cheese slices on a plate, turned her around, and kissed her on the mouth.

"I'm glad I did, too," he said.

Rosalie was astonished. What a crazy afternoon! It would make a good story, but she certainly wasn't going to tell Judy *this* part of it. She smiled at Ed. "You're acting pretty romantic," she said. The word just seemed to pop out before she could stop it.

Ed stepped back, looking embarrassed. "Here's your mom," he said.

Rita came into the kitchen, loaded down with shopping bags. "Hi, Ed. Nice to see ya, it's been a long time. Hi, hon—" She let the bags down onto a chair and looked around. "Rosalie! It looks beautiful in here! What a sight for sore eyes!" She ran into the living room.

Rosalie and Ed smiled at each other.

Rita came back into the kitchen and hugged Rosalie. "The house is beautiful, hon! You must've been working hard all day!"

"Not that hard," Rosalie said. "How about you?"

"Wait'll I show you all the things I bought!" Rita began to open her bags. She pulled out a piece of flowered material, and held it up. "Look at this, for little wrappers. And this flannel, that was on sale. And just wait—" She pulled at the string around the biggest package. "How about this, for the carriage?" She held up a ruffled pillow with the word *Baby* stenciled on it. "I'm gonna embroider that up with little flowers all around it, won't that be something?"

"That's nice, Mom," Rosalie said. Out of the corner of her eye she saw the VW pull in next door. "The supper's ready," she said. "It's just sandwiches, I hope that's O.K."

"It looks real nice," Rita said. She washed her hands at the sink, then sat down. "They had these books at the store," she said, pulling a pamphlet out of one of the bags. "How to name the baby." She opened it and began to read. " 'Abner, Alan, Alexandra—' "

"Alexandra's pretty," Rosalie said. It made the baby seem very real to talk like this.

"Not as pretty as Rosalie!" Rita said immediately.

"Yeah, Rosalie's the best name, I think," Ed put in, smiling at her.

They began to eat. From next door, Rosalie could hear Tony and Jill talking, and the clinking sound of garden tools. They must be putting in the flowers, she thought. But she didn't look out.

"What time are you two going out?" Rita asked over coffee.

Ed looked at the clock. "We should go! The rehearsal's supposed to start early, at seven."

Rosalie pushed her chair back. "Don't bother to clean up, Mom. I'll do it when I come home."

Rita sat back in her chair and smiled at them. "You kids have a nice time. Don't stay late," she added, automatically.

"There might be a party afterward," Rosalie said.

"There is," Ed told her. "It's at Billy Kirchener's. He said we should come."

"Can I, Mom?"

"Sure," Rita said. "You kids go out and have yourselves a nice time. I'm gonna go out to Bingo with Maxine, anyway."

Rosalie and Ed went to the door. Outside, Jill and Tony sat on the trailer steps. They had planted the flowers; a forlorn row of them straggled in the bare dirt.

Jill waved. "Hi, Rosie. Want to come over a while?"

Rosalie waved back. "We can't," she called. "We're going out."

18

Rosalie walked across the parking lot, blinking in the hot sun that beat down on the cars and melted the tar in the cracked surface. Every few steps, her new sandals stuck to a soft spot.

She reached the sidewalk and walked in the thin strip of shade under the canvas awnings, watching her dark reflection move across the store windows. The shadow looked tall and mysterious.

She pushed through the door of Loretta's and was hit by the rush of air conditioning inside, the sound of it almost covering the hum of hair dryers and the beat of radio music.

Rita was at her station, combing out a hairdo and laughing with Maxine, who stood behind the next chair. Unaware of Rosalie, they chatted and joked. Rosalie stood inside the door and watched them. I wouldn't want to work here, she thought. But wherever I end up, I hope it's as friendly as this.

Rita noticed her and looked up. "Look who's here," she said to Maxine.

Maxine, who was placing a roller deftly in a customer's hair, turned around.

"Hi, kid!" she called over to Rosalie. "All set for the big change? I'm gonna be with you in one minute."

"Ready, I guess," Rosalie said. She sat on the bench by the window and looked at the customers. They all seemed half asleep in the cool flow of air.

Doreen came out of the back room with a broom and dustpan. "Rosalie!" she cried. "I almost didn't recognize you. You look terrific! Did you lose weight?"

"Yeah. I've been on a diet."

"Well, congratulations!" Doreen patted her thin midriff. "I wish I had your willpower. I'm never going to fit into my last year's bikini the way I am now."

"Doreen, don't be crazy! You're skinny as a rail." Rosalie had always hated talking about weight with thin people. But now she didn't seem to mind.

"Get the kid a cape, will ya, Doreen?" Maxine called, helping her customer out of the chair. "O.K., Rosie, come on over. I'm ready and waiting."

She brushed some hair off the seat and waved Rosalie onto it. Doreen unfolded a pink cape and tied it under Rosalie's hair.

Rita smiled over at her. "That's my girl," she told her customer. "Rosalie. She's having her hair cut short. I can't wait to see what Maxine's gonna do with it."

The woman looked curiously at Rosalie. "I didn't know you had a girl this big, Rita."

"Yep, she's gonna be in ninth grade next fall, how about that?" Rita said. "Taking the academic program. Who knows, she might end up a teacher or something. She's got a good job baby-sitting this summer."

"A nice tall girl like that, she could be a model," the customer said.

Rosalie didn't mind the compliment, but she knew she would hate being a model. It would be so boring, compared to working with people. She shifted anxiously in the chair, watching Maxine lay out scissors and clips.

"Getting nervous?" Maxine began to brush her hair.

"Sort of." She didn't want to say how much the haircut meant to her. It was like cutting herself off from the way she used to be. Changing. Not because her mother nagged her into it, but because she was ready.

"Believe me, you don't have a thing to worry about. You're gonna walk out of here gorgeous, I promise you." Maxine put the brush down and reached for a comb. "Get this mop of hair off you, you're gonna feel like a million dollars." She combed through Rosalie's hair with sure, gentle strokes.

Rosalie relaxed, staring dreamily at her reflection in the mirror as Maxine combed her hair over her shoulders. For just an instant she felt regretful; right now her hair looked nicer than it had for months. She reached up to touch it cautiously.

"Change your mind?" Maxine laughed.

"No. Go ahead."

All of a sudden she couldn't wait. She held her breath as Maxine clipped the back hair to the top of her head, picked up a strand from the front, studied it thoughtfully and snipped it off.

The hair fell to the floor.

Doreen came up behind them. "That's wonderful hair," she said. "So nice and thick."

Rita watched anxiously. "Take it easy, Maxine! Not *too* short!"

"Mom!" Rosalie tensed up.

"Who's giving this haircut, Rita, you or me?" Maxine demanded, smiling. She snipped another chunk. "You take this kid to some fancy New York salon, they'd ask fifty dollars for a cut like I'm gonna give her right here." She pointed beyond Rita's customer. "See that picture up there? That's the latest style, right out of this month's *Hairdo* magazine. Every society woman on Fifth Avenue's gonna have her hair cut like this by next week."

Rosalie stared into the mirror. Half her hair was short.

She looked like a Before and After picture, all at once.

Doreen had perched on the bench and was flipping through a fashion magazine. "It looks like half the models in here don't even have a bra on," she said. "You can see everything right through their clothes."

Rita straightened up. "I don't know what's left—show them topless, that's about it." She twirled her customer around and held a mirror to the back of her head. The woman nodded complacently, patting her hair.

Rita went on. "Remember the bras they used to have when we were kids, Maxine? I'm telling you, no girl would of even thought about burning a bra back then, when it was one of those cute little numbers with the lace and the wires to push you out so you looked like Marilyn Monroe, even if you were flat as a board."

"That's right," Maxine said, snipping carefully. "Those wires just about killed you in the heat, remember? Like steel bands right across your chest. I used to think I would faint."

Rita laughed.

Her customer picked up. "Remember those Merry Widow waist-cinchers with the garters hanging down? I wore one of them under a strapless formal to a dance one time. I didn't faint, but I had to sit down and catch my breath after each number. Oh, my, those were the days."

"The good old days." Maxine squinted at Rosalie's head. "I can't say I miss them." She pushed Rosalie's head down and snipped at the back of her neck. "All that growing up, it's not easy. Right, Rosie?"

"I guess so," Rosalie said, agreeing fervently in her heart. It isn't easy, she thought. It's awfully complicated. And it takes so long.

Maxine began to snip across Rosalie's forehead. "We're

getting there. Just a couple more minutes, then I'll brush it out and you'll see the new you."

Rita's customer stuffed a bill into the pocket of her uniform. "Thanks, Rita. It looks real nice." She climbed out of the chair and went to the desk to pay Doreen.

Rita put her combs and clips away and sat down in her chair, her legs stretched out in front of her, watching Maxine.

"Maxine, you're a wonder. She's gonna look beautiful!"

Maxine put down her scissors and began to brush Rosalie's hair. "Wait a sec, don't look yet," she cautioned. She brushed Rosalie's bangs, shaped the sides with her hands, untied Rosalie's cape, wiped her neck, and stood back, waiting.

"O.K. Whaddya say?"

Rosalie looked straight into the mirror. Fluffy curls framed her face. She reached up to feel them, smiling shyly at the new reflection. The dark-eyed girl in the mirror stared back at her. Rosalie looked at her, unsure.

"The new you," Maxine announced.

Rosalie tilted her head. She looked so different! She could hardly remember the way she had looked when she came in.

"Well?" Maxine asked, beaming.

"Oh, Maxine—" Rosalie said. She wondered what Tony and Jill would think. Then she realized that it didn't matter as much now. "I think it's terrific!" she said. She got out of the chair and hugged Maxine. "Thanks! Thanks a lot!"

"Any time," Maxine said, smiling.

"That is gorgeous," Doreen said.

Rita circled around Rosalie, looking at her from all sides. "I knew it," she said. "I just knew it. I kept telling you, didn't I, Rosalie? That's just a beautiful cut, and it's gonna practically take care of itself." She smiled triumphantly at Maxine. "I guess that'll teach her to listen to us from now on!"

Rosalie hugged her mother. Let her think it was all her idea; she didn't care. "I love it, Mom."

She pulled open the door and went out, leaving the smell of hair spray behind her. She felt giddy and light-headed and very new.

BETTY MILES is the author of a wide range of popular books for young readers, including *Just Think!*, a book about concepts, *Save The Earth!*, an ecology handbook, and *Around and Around—Love*, a photo-essay. Her novels include *The Real Me, Just the Beginning* and, most recently, *All It Takes Is Practice.*

Betty Miles teaches children's literature at Bank Street College of Education in New York City, and is a frequent contributor to magazines. She lives with her husband in Rockland County, New York. They have three grown children.